From Lisa —
Mother's Day 2012

P9-DXE-721

For One More Day

For One More Day

Mitch Albom

GIFT BOOKS

"Let me guess. You want to know why I tried to kill myself."

—Chick Benetto's first words to me

*T*HIS IS A STORY ABOUT A FAMILY and, as there is a ghost involved, you might call it a ghost story. But every family is a ghost story. The dead sit at our tables long after they have gone.

THIS PARTICULAR STORY belongs to Charles "Chick" Benetto. He was not the ghost. He was very real. I found him on a Saturday morning, in the bleachers of a Little League field, wearing a navy windbreaker and chewing peppermint gum. Maybe you remember him from his baseball days. I have spent part of my career as a sportswriter, so the name was familiar to me on several levels.

Looking back, it was fate that I found him. I had come to Pepperville Beach to close on a small house that had been in our family for years. On my way back to the airport, I stopped for coffee. There was a field across the street where kids in purple t-shirts were pitching and hitting. I had time. I wandered over.

As I stood at the backstop, my fingers curled in the chain-link fence, an old man maneuvered a lawn mower over the grass. He was tanned and wrinkled, with half a cigar in his mouth. He shut the mower when he saw me and asked if

I had a kid out there. I said no. He asked what I was doing here. I told him about the house. He asked what I did for a living and I made the mistake of telling him that, too.

"A writer, huh?" he said, chewing his cigar. He pointed to a figure sitting alone in the seats with his back to us. "You oughta check out that guy. Now *there's* a story."

I hear this all the time.

"Oh, yeah? Why's that?"

"He played pro ball once."

"Mm-hmm."

"I think he made a World Series."

"Mmm."

"And he tried to kill himself."

"What?"

"Yeah." The man sniffed. "From what I heard, he's damn lucky to be alive. Chick Benetto, his name is. His mother used to live around here. Posey Benetto." He chuckled. "She was wild."

He dropped his cigar and stomped on it. "Go on up and ask him if you don't believe me."

He returned to his mower. I let go of the fence. It was rusty, and some of the rust came off on my fingers.

Every family is a ghost story.

I approached the bleachers.

ⲟⲝ WHAT I HAVE written here is what Charles "Chick" Benetto told me in our conversation that morning—which stretched out much longer than that—as well as personal notes and pages from his journal that I found later, on my own. I have assembled them into the following narrative, in his voice, because I'm not sure you would believe this story if you *didn't* hear it in his voice.

You may not believe it anyhow.

But ask yourself this: Have you ever lost someone you love and wanted one more conversation, one more chance to make up for the time when you thought they would be here forever? If so, then you know you can go your whole life collecting days, and none will outweigh the one you wish you had back.

What if you got it back?

May 2006

I. Midnight

Chick's Story

*L*ET ME GUESS. You want to know why I tried to kill myself.

You want to know how I survived. Why I disappeared. Where I've been all this time. But first, why I tried to kill myself, right?

It's OK. People do. They measure themselves against me. It's like this line is drawn somewhere in the world and if you never cross it, you'll never consider throwing yourself off a building or swallowing a bottle of pills—but if you do, you might. People figure I crossed the line. They ask themselves, "Could I ever get as close as *he* did?"

The truth is, there is no line. There's only your life, how you mess it up, and who is there to save you.

Or who isn't.

℘ LOOKING BACK, I began to unravel the day my mother died, around ten years ago. I wasn't there when it happened, and I should have been. So I lied. That was a bad idea. A funeral is no place for secrets. I stood by her gravesite trying to believe it wasn't my fault, and then my fourteen-year-old daughter took my hand and whispered, "I'm sorry you didn't get a chance to say good-bye, Dad," and that was it. I broke down. I fell to my knees, crying, the wet grass staining my pants.

After the funeral, I got so drunk I passed out on our couch. And something changed. One day can bend your life, and that day seemed to bend mine inexorably downward. My mother had been all over me as a kid—advice, criticism, the whole smothering mothering thing. There were times I wished she would leave me alone.

But then she did. She died. No more visits, no more phone calls. And without even realizing it, I began to drift, as if my roots had been pulled, as if I were floating down some side branch of a river. Mothers support certain illusions about their children, and one of my illusions was that I liked who I was, because she did. When she passed away, so did that idea.

The truth is, I didn't like who I was at all. In my mind, I still pictured myself a promising, young athlete. But I was no longer young and I was no longer an athlete. I was a middle-aged salesman. My promise had long since passed.

A year after my mother died, I did the dumbest thing I've ever done financially. I let a saleswoman talk me into an investment scheme. She was young and good-looking in that confident, breezy, two-buttons-undone fashion that makes an older man feel bitter when she walks past him—unless, of course, she speaks to him. Then he gets stupid. We met three times to discuss the proposal: twice at her office, once in a Greek restaurant, nothing improper, but by the time her perfume cleared my head, I'd put most of my savings in a now-worthless stock fund. She quickly got "transferred" to the West Coast. I had to explain to my wife, Catherine, where the money went.

After that, I drank more—ballplayers in my time always drank—but it became a problem which, in time, got me fired from two sales jobs. And getting fired made me keep on drinking. I slept badly. I ate badly. I seemed to be aging while standing still. When I did find work, I hid mouthwash and eyedrops in my pockets, darting into bathrooms before meeting clients. Money became a problem; Catherine and I fought constantly about it. And, over time, our marriage collapsed. She grew tired of my misery and I can't say I blame her. When you're rotten about yourself, you become rotten to everyone else, even those you love. One night she found me passed out on the basement floor with my lip cut, cradling a baseball glove.

I left my family shortly thereafter—or they left me.

I am more ashamed of that than I can say.

I moved to an apartment. I grew ornery and distant. I avoided anyone who wouldn't drink with me. My mother, had she been alive, might have found a way through to me because she was always good at that, taking my arm and saying, "Come on, Charley, what's the story?" But she wasn't around, and that's the thing when your parents die, you feel like instead of going into every fight with backup, you are going into every fight alone.

And one night, in early October, I decided to kill myself.

Maybe you're surprised. Maybe you figure men like me, men who play in a World Series, can never sink as low as suicide because they always have, at the very least, that "dream came true" thing. But you'd be wrong. All that happens when your dream comes true is a slow, melting realization that it wasn't what you thought.

And it won't save you.

☙ WHAT FINISHED ME, what pushed me over the edge, strange as it sounds, was my daughter's wedding. She was twenty-two now, with long, straight hair, chestnut-colored, like her mother's, and the same full lips. She married a "wonderful guy" in an afternoon ceremony.

And that's all I know because that's all she wrote, in a brief letter which arrived at my apartment a few weeks after the event.

Apparently, through my drinking, depression, and generally bad behavior, I had become too great an embarrassment to risk at a family function. Instead, I received that letter and two photographs, one of my daughter and her new husband, hands clasped, standing under a tree; the other of the happy couple toasting with champagne.

It was the second photo that broke me. One of those candid snapshots that catches a moment never to be repeated, the two of them laughing in midsentence, tipping their glasses. It was so innocent and so young and so . . . past tense. It seemed to taunt my absence. *And you weren't there.* I didn't even know this guy. My ex-wife did. Our old friends did. *And you weren't there.* Once again, I had been absent from a critical family moment. This time, my little girl would not take my hand and comfort me; she belonged to someone else. I was not being asked. I was being notified.

I looked at the envelope, which carried her new last name (*Maria Lang*, not *Maria Benetto*) and no return address (Why? Were they afraid I might visit them?), and something sunk so low inside me I couldn't find it anymore. You get shut out of your only child's life, you feel like a steel door has been locked; you're banging, but they just can't hear you. And being unheard is the ground floor of giving up, and giving up is the ground floor of doing yourself in.

So I tried to.

It's not so much, what's the point? It's more like what's the difference?

When he went blundering back to God,
His songs half written, his work half done,
Who knows what paths his bruised feet trod,
What hills of peace or pain he won?

I hope God smiled and took his hand,
And said, "Poor truant, passionate fool!
Life's book is hard to understand:
Why couldst thou not remain at school?"

(a poem, by Charles Hanson Towne,
found inside a notebook amongst
Chick Benetto's belongings)

Chick Tries to End It All

*T*HAT LETTER FROM MY DAUGHTER arrived on a Friday, which conveniently allowed for a weekend bender, not much of which I remember. Monday morning, despite a long, cold shower, I was two hours late for work. When I got to the office, I lasted less than forty-five minutes. My head was throbbing. The place felt like a tomb. I slid into the Xerox room, then the bathroom, then the elevator, without a coat or a briefcase, so that, if someone were charting my movements, they would seem normal and not an orchestrated exit.

That was stupid. No one cared. This was a big company with lots of salespeople and it could survive just fine without me, as we now know, since that walk from the elevator to the parking lot was my last act as an employee.

NEXT, I CALLED my ex-wife. I called from a pay phone. She was at work.

"Why?" I said when she answered.

"Chick?"

"Why?" I repeated. I'd had three days to lather up my anger, and that was all that came out. One word. "Why?"

"Chick." Her tone softened.

"I wasn't even *invited*?"

"It was their idea. They thought it was . . ."

"What? Safer? I was going to do something?"

"I don't know—"

"I'm a monster now? Is that it?"

"Where are you?"

"I'm a monster?"

"Stop."

"I'm leaving."

"Look, Chick, she's not a kid anymore, and if—"

"You couldn't stand up for me?"

I heard her exhale.

"Leaving where?" she said.

"You couldn't stand up for me?"

"I'm sorry. It's complicated. There's his family, too. And they—"

"Did you go with someone?"

"Oh, Chick . . . I'm at work, OK?"

At that moment, I felt lonelier than I'd ever felt before, and that loneliness seemed to squat in my lungs and crush all but my most minimal breathing. There was nothing left to say. Not about this. Not about anything.

"It's all right," I whispered. "I'm sorry."

There was a pause.

"Leaving where?" she said.

I hung up.

ᘒᘒ AND THEN, FOR the last time, I got drunk. First at a place called Mr. Ted's Pub, where the bartender was a skinny, round-faced kid, probably no older than the guy my daughter married. Later I went back to my apartment and drank some more. I knocked over furniture. I wrote on the walls. I think I actually stuffed the wedding photos down the garbage disposal. Somewhere in the middle of the night I decided to go home, meaning Pepperville Beach, the town where I grew up. It was two hours away by car, but I hadn't been there in years. I moved around my apartment, walking in circles as if preparing for the journey. You don't need much for a good-bye trip. I went to the bedroom and took a gun out of the drawer.

I stumbled down to the garage, found my car, put the gun in the glove compartment, threw a jacket in the backseat, maybe the front seat, or maybe the jacket was already there, I don't know, and I screeched into the street. The city was quiet, the lights were blinking yellow, and I was going to end my life where I began it.

Blundering back to God. Simple as that.

We are proud to announce the birth of

Charles Alexander

8 pounds, 11 ounces

November 21, 1949

Leonard and Pauline Benetto

(from Chick Benetto's papers)

*I*T WAS COLD AND RAINING LIGHTLY, but the highway was empty, and I used every one of its four lanes, weaving back and forth. You would think, you would hope, that someone as lit as I was would be stopped by the police, but I wasn't. At one point I even rolled into one of those all-night convenience stores, and I bought a six-pack of beer from an Asian guy with a thin mustache.

"Lottery ticket?" he asked.

I had, over the years, perfected a functional appearance when I was smashed—the alcoholic as walking man—and I pretended to give the question some thought.

"Not this time," I said.

He put the beer in a bag. I caught his gaze, two dull, dark eyes, and I thought to myself, *This is the last face I will see on earth.*

He pushed my change across the counter.

BY THE TIME I saw the sign for my hometown—PEPPERVILLE BEACH, EXIT 1 MILE—two of the beers were gone, and one had spilled all over the passenger seat. The wipers were thumping. I was fighting to stay awake. I must have tranced out thinking, "Exit 1 Mile," because after a while I saw a sign for another town and realized I had missed my turnoff altogether. I banged on the dashboard. Then I spun the car around, right there, in the middle of the highway, and drove back in the wrong direction. There was no traffic and I wouldn't have cared anyhow. I was getting to that exit. I slammed the accelerator. Quickly enough, a ramp came into view—the on-ramp, not the exit ramp—and I screeched toward it. It was one of those long twisting things, and I held the wheel in a locked turn, going fast, around and down.

Suddenly, two huge lights blinded me, like two giant suns. Then a truck horn blasted, then a jolting smash, then my car flew over an embankment and landed hard, thumping downhill. There was glass everywhere and beer cans bouncing around and I grabbed wildly at the steering wheel and the car jerked backward, flipping me onto my stomach. I somehow found the door handle and yanked it hard, and I remember flashes of black sky and green weeds and a sound like thunder and something high and solid crashing down.

രൂ WHEN I OPENED my eyes, I was lying in wet grass. My car was half-buried under a now-destroyed billboard for a local Chevrolet dealership, into which it had apparently plowed. In one of those freak moments of physics, I must have been thrown from the vehicle before its final impact. I can't explain it. When you want to die, you are spared. Who can explain that?

I slowly, painfully, got to my feet. My back was soaked. I ached all over. It was still raining lightly, but it was quiet, save for the sound of crickets. Normally, at this point, you'd say, "I was just happy to be alive," but I can't say that, because I wasn't. I looked up at the highway. In the mist, I could make out the truck, like a big, hulking shipwreck, the front cab bent as if its neck had been snapped. Steam rose from the hood. One headlamp was still working, casting a lonely beam down the muddy hill that made twinkling diamonds out of the shattered glass.

Where was the driver? Was he alive? Hurt? Bleeding? Breathing? The courageous thing, of course, would have been to climb up and check, but courage was not my strong suit at that moment.

So I didn't.

Instead, I put my hands down flat by my sides and I turned south, walking back toward my old town. I am not proud of this. But I was not in any way rational. I was a zombie, a robot, devoid of concern for anyone, myself included—myself, actually, at the top of the list. I forgot about the car, the truck, the gun; I left it all behind. My shoes crunched on the gravel, and I heard the crickets laughing.

———

ﻌ I CAN'T SAY how long I walked. Long enough that the rain stopped and the sky began to lighten with the first stirrings of dawn. I reached the outskirts of Pepperville Beach, which was marked by a big, rusty water tower, just behind the baseball fields. In small towns like mine, climbing water towers was a rite of passage, and my baseball buddies and I used to climb this one on weekends, the spray-paint cans jammed in our waistbands.

Now I stood before that water tower again, wet and old and broken and drunk and perhaps a killer, I should add, or so I suspected, because I never did see the driver of the truck. It didn't matter, because my next act was a no-brainer, as determined as I was to make this the last night of my life.

I found the ladder's bottom.

I began to climb.

It took me a while to reach the riveted tank. When I finally did, I collapsed on the catwalk, breathing hard, sucking air. In the back of my addled brain, a voice scolded me for being so out of shape.

I looked out on the trees below me. Behind them I saw the baseball field where I had learned the game from my father. The sight of it still dredged up sad memories. What is it about childhood that never lets you go, even when you're so wrecked it's hard to believe you ever *were* a child?

The sky was lightening. The crickets grew louder. I had a sudden memory flash of little Maria asleep on my chest when she was small enough to cradle in one arm, her skin smelling of talcum powder. Then I had a vision of me, wet and filthy as I was now, bursting into her wedding, the music stopping, everyone looking up horrified, Maria the most horrified of all.

I lowered my head.

I would not be missed.

I took two running steps, grabbed the railing, and hurled myself over.

ﮩ THE REST IS inexplicable. What I hit, how I survived, I cannot tell you. All I recall is twisting and snapping and brushing and flipping and scraping and a final thud. These scars on my face? I figured they came from that. It seemed as if I fell for a very long time.

When I opened my eyes, I was surrounded by fallen pieces of the tree. Stones pressed into my stomach and chest. I lifted my chin, and this is what I saw: the baseball field of my youth, coming into the morning light, the two dugouts, the pitcher's mound.

And my mother, who had been dead for years.

II. Morning

Chick's Mom

My FATHER ONCE TOLD ME, "You can be a mama's boy or a daddy's boy. But you can't be both."

So I was a daddy's boy. I mimicked his walk. I mimicked his deep, smoky laugh. I carried a baseball glove because he loved baseball, and I took every hardball he threw, even the ones that stung my hands so badly I thought I would scream.

When school was out, I would run to his liquor store on Kraft Avenue and stay until dinnertime, playing with empty boxes in the storeroom, waiting for him to finish. We would ride home together in his sky blue Buick sedan, and sometimes we would sit in the driveway as he smoked his Chesterfields and listened to the radio news.

I have a younger sister named Roberta, and back then she wore pink ballerina slippers almost everywhere. When we ate at the local diner, my mother would yank her to the "ladies' " room—her pink feet sliding across the tile—while my father took me to the "gents'." In my young mind I figured this was life's assignment: me with him, her with her. Ladies'. Gents'. Mama's. Daddy's.

A daddy's boy.

I was a daddy's boy, and I remained a daddy's boy right up to a hot, cloudless Saturday morning in the spring of my fifth grade year. We had a doubleheader scheduled that day against the Cardinals, who wore red wool uniforms and were sponsored by Connor's Plumbing Supply.

The sun was already warming the kitchen when I entered in my long socks, carrying my glove, and saw my mother at the table smoking a cigarette. My mother was a beautiful woman, but she didn't look beautiful that morning. She bit her lip and looked away from me. I remember the smell of burnt toast and I thought she was upset because she messed up breakfast.

"I'll eat cereal," I said.

I took a bowl from the cupboard.

She cleared her throat. "What time is your game, honey?"

"Do you have a cold?" I asked.

She shook her head and put a hand to her cheek. "What time is your game?"

"I dunno." I shrugged. This was before I wore a watch.

I got the glass bottle of milk and the big box of corn puffs. I poured the corn puffs too fast and some bounced out of the bowl and onto the table. My mother picked them up, one at a time, and put them in her palm.

"I'll take you," she whispered. "Whenever it is."

"Why can't Daddy take me?" I asked.

"Daddy's not here."

"Where is he?"

She didn't answer.

"When's he coming back?"

She squeezed the corn puffs and they crumbled into floury dust.

I was a mama's boy from that day on.

NOW, WHEN I SAW MY DEAD MOTHER, I mean just that. I saw her. She was standing by the dugout, wearing a lavender jacket, holding her pocketbook. She didn't say a word. She just looked at me.

I tried to lift myself in her direction then fell back, a bolt of pain shooting through my muscles. My brain wanted to shout her name, but there was no sound from my throat.

I lowered my head and put my palms together. I pushed hard again, and this time I lifted myself halfway off the ground. I looked up.

She was gone.

I don't expect you to go with me here. It's crazy, I know. You don't see dead people. You don't get visits. You don't fall off of a water tower, miraculously alive despite your best attempt to kill yourself, and see your dearly departed mother holding her pocketbook on the third-base line.

I have given it all the thought that you are probably giving it right now; a hallucination, a fantasy, a drunken dream, the mixed-up brain on its mixed-up way. As I say, I don't expect you to go with me here.

But this is what happened. She had been there. I had seen her. I lay on the field for an indeterminate amount of time, then I rose to my feet and I got myself walking. I brushed the sand and debris from my knees and forearms. I was bleeding from dozens of cuts, most of them small, a few bigger. I could taste blood in my mouth.

I cut across a familiar patch of grass. A morning wind shook the trees and brought a sweep of yellow leaves, like a small, fluttering rainstorm. I had twice failed to kill myself. How pathetic was that?

I headed toward my old house, determined to finish the job.

Dear Charley—

Have lots of FUN in SCHOOL today!

I will see you at lunchtime and we'll get a milkshake.

I love you every day!

Mom

(from Chick Benetto's papers, circa 1954)

How Mother Met Father

*M*Y MOTHER WAS ALWAYS WRITING ME NOTES. She slipped them to me whenever she dropped me off somewhere. I never understood this, since anything she had to say she could have said right then and saved herself the paper and the awful taste of envelope glue.

I think the first note was on my first day of kindergarten in 1954. What was I, five years old? The schoolyard was filled with kids, shrieking and running around. We approached, me holding my mother's hand, as a woman in a black beret formed lines in front of the teachers. I saw the other mothers kissing their kids and walking away. I must have started crying.

"What's the matter?" my mother asked.

"Don't go."

"I'll be here when you come out."

"No."

"It's OK. I'll be here."

"What if I can't find you?"

"You will."

"What if I lose you?"

"You can't lose your mother, Charley."

She smiled. She reached inside her jacket pocket and handed me a small blue envelope.

"Here," she said. "If you miss me really badly, you can open this."

She wiped my eyes with a tissue from her purse, then hugged me good-bye. I can still see her walking backward, blowing me kisses, her lips painted in red Revlon, her hair swept up above her ears. I waved good-bye with the letter. It didn't occur to her, I guess, that I was just starting school and didn't know how to read. That was my mother. It was the thought that counted.

SHE MET MY father, the story goes, down by Pepperville Lake in the spring of 1944. She was swimming and he was throwing a baseball with his friend, and his friend whipped it too high and it landed in the water. My mother swam to get it. My father splashed in. As he surfaced with the ball, they banged heads.

"And we never stopped," she would say.

They had a fast, intense courtship, because that's how my father was, he started things with an aim to finish them. He was a tall, meaty young man, fresh out of high school, who combed his hair in a high pompadour and drove his father's blue-and-white LaSalle. He enlisted in World War II as soon as he could, telling my mother he'd like to "kill more of the enemy than anyone in our town." He was shipped overseas to Italy, the northern Apennine mountains and the Po

Valley, near Bologna. In a letter from there, in 1945, he proposed to my mother. "Be my wife," he wrote, which sounded more like a command to me. My mother agreed in a return letter she wrote on special linen stationery, which was too expensive for her but which she bought anyhow, my mother being respectful of both words and the vehicle used to deliver them.

Two weeks after my father received it, the Germans signed the surrender documents. He was coming home.

My theory was he never got enough war for his liking. So he made his own with us.

☙ MY FATHER'S NAME was Leonard, but everyone called him Len, and my mother's name was Pauline, but everyone called her "Posey," like the nursery rhyme, "a pocketful of Posey." She had large, almond-shaped eyes, dark, sweeping hair that she often wore up, and a soft, creamy complexion. She reminded people of the actress Audrey Hepburn, and in our small town, there weren't many women who fit that description. She loved wearing makeup—mascara, eyeliner, rouge, you name it—and while most people considered her "fun" or "perky" or, later, "eccentric" or "headstrong," for most of my childhood I considered her a nag.

Was I wearing my galoshes? Did I have my jacket? Did I finish my schoolwork? Why were my pants ripped?

She was always correcting my grammar.

"Me and Roberta are gonna—," I'd start.

"Roberta and *I*," she would interrupt.

"Me and Jimmy want to—"

"Jimmy and *I*," she would say.

Parents slot into postures in a child's mind, and my mother's posture was a lipsticked woman leaning over, wagging a finger, imploring me to be better than I was. My father's posture was a man in repose, shoulders pressed against a wall, holding a cigarette, watching me sink or swim.

In retrospect, I should have made more of the fact that one was leaning toward me and the other was leaning away. But I was a kid, and what do kids know?

 MY MOTHER WAS French Protestant, and my father was Italian Catholic, and their union was an excess of God, guilt, and sauce. They argued all the time. The kids. Food. Religion. My father would hang a picture of Jesus on the wall outside the bathroom and, while he was at work, my mother would move it somewhere less conspicuous. He would come home and yell, "You can't move Jesus, for Christ's sake!" and she would say, "It's a picture, Len. You think God wants to hang by the bathroom?"

And he would put it back.

And the next day she would move it.

On and on like that.

They were a blend of backgrounds and cultures, but if my family was a democracy, my father's vote counted twice.

He decided what we should eat for dinner, what color to paint the house, which bank we should use, which channel we watched on our Zenith console black-and-white TV set. On the day I was born, he informed my mother, "The kid is getting baptized in the Catholic church," and that was that.

The funny thing is, he wasn't religious himself. After the war, my father, who owned a liquor store, was more interested in profits than prophecies. And when it came to me, the only thing I had to worship was baseball. He was pitching to me before I could walk. He gave me a wooden bat before my mother let me use scissors. He said I could make the major leagues one day if I had "a plan," and if I "stuck to the plan."

Of course, when you're that young, you nest in your parents' plans, not your own.

And so, from the time I was seven years old, I scanned the newspaper for the box scores of my future employers. I kept a glove at my father's liquor store in case he could steal a few minutes and throw to me in the parking lot. I even wore cleats to Sunday mass sometimes, because we left for American Legion games right after the final hymn. When they referred to the church as "God's house," I worried that the Lord did not appreciate my spikes digging into his floors. I tried standing on my toes once but my father whispered, "What the hell are you doing?" and I lowered myself quickly.

―――――――

◎∽ MY MOTHER, ON the other hand, didn't care for base-ball. She'd been an only child, her family had been poor, and she'd had to drop out of school to work during the war. She earned her high school diploma at night, and did nursing school after that. In her mind, for me, there were only books and college and the gates they would open. The best she could say about baseball was that it "gets you some fresh air."

But she showed up. She sat in the stands, wearing her big sunglasses, her hair well coiffed, courtesy of the local beauty parlor. Sometimes I would peek at her from inside the dugout, and she'd be looking off over the horizon. But when I came to bat, she clapped and yelled, "Yaaay, Charley!" and I guess that's all I cared about. My father, who coached every team I played on up to the day he split, once caught me look-ing her way and hollered, "Eyes on the ball, Chick! There's nothing up there that's gonna help you!"

Mom, I guess, wasn't part of "the plan."

◎∽ STILL, I CAN say I adored my mother, in the way that boys adore their mothers while taking them for granted. She made that easy. For one thing, she was funny. She didn't mind smearing ice cream on her face for a laugh. She did odd voices, like Popeye the Sailor Man, or Louis Armstrong croaking, "If ya ain't got it in ya, ya can't blow it out." She tickled me and she let me tickle her back, squeezing her elbows in as she laughed. She tucked me in every night, rubbing my hair and saying, "Give your mother a kiss." She told me I was smart and that being smart was a privilege, and she insisted that I read one book every week, and took me to the library to make sure this happened. She dressed too flashy sometimes, and she sang along with our music, which bothered me. But there was never, not for a moment, a question of trust between us.

If my mother said it, I believed it.

She wasn't easy on me, don't get me wrong. She smacked me. She scolded me. She punished me. But she loved me. She really did. She loved me falling off a swing set. She loved me stepping on her floors with muddy shoes. She loved me through vomit and snot and bloody knees. She loved me coming and going, at my worst and at my best. She had a bottomless well of love for me.

Her only flaw was that she didn't make me work for it.

You see, here's my theory: Kids chase the love that eludes them, and for me, that was my father's love. He kept it tucked away, like papers in a briefcase. And I kept trying to get in there.

Years later, after her death, I made lists of Times My Mother Stood Up for Me and Times I Did Not Stand Up for My Mother. It was sad, the imbalance of it all. Why do kids assume so much from one parent and hold the other to a lower, looser standard?

Maybe it's like my old man said: You can be a mama's boy or a daddy's boy, but you can't be both. So you cling to the one you think you might lose.

Times My Mother Stood Up for Me

I am five years old. We are walking to Fanelli's market. A neighbor in a bathrobe and pink curlers opens her screen door and calls to my mother. As they talk, I wander to the backyard of the house next door.

Suddenly, out of nowhere, a German shepherd lunges at me. Awowwow! *It is tethered to a clothesline.* Awowwow! *It rises on its hind legs, straining the leash.* Awowwowow!

I whirl and run. I am screaming. My mother dashes to me. "What?" she hollers, grabbing my elbows. "What is it?" "A dog!" She exhales. "A dog? Where? Around there?" I nod, crying.

She marches me around the house. There is the dog. It howls again. Awowwowowow! *I jump back. But my mother yanks me forward. And she barks. She barks. She makes the best barking sound I have ever heard a human being make.*

The dog falls into a whimpering crouch. My mother turns. "You have to show them who's boss, Charley," she says.

(from a list in a notebook found amongst Chick Benetto's belongings)

Chick Returns to His Old House

*B*Y NOW, THE MORNING SUN was just over the horizon and it came at me like a sidearm pitch between the houses of my old neighborhood. I shielded my eyes. This being early October, there were already piles of leaves pushed against the curb—more leaves than I remembered from my autumns here—and less open space in the sky. I think what you notice most when you haven't been home in a while is how much the trees have grown around your memories.

Pepperville Beach. Do you know how it got its name? It's almost embarrassing. A small patch of sand had been trucked in years ago by some entrepreneur who thought the town would be more impressive if we had a beach, even though we didn't have an ocean. He joined the chamber of commerce and he even got the town's name changed—Pepperville Lake became Pepperville Beach—despite the fact that our "beach" had a swing set and a sliding board and was big enough for about twelve families before you'd be sitting on someone else's towel. It became a sort of joke when we were growing up—"Hey, you wanna go to the *beach*?" or "Hey, it looks like a *beach* day to me"—because we knew we weren't fooling anybody.

Anyhow, our house was near the lake—and the "beach"—and my sister and I had kept it after our mother died because I guess we hoped it might be worth something someday. To be honest, I didn't have the stomach to sell it.

Now I walked toward that house with my back hunched like a fugitive. I had left the scene of an accident and surely someone had discovered the car, the truck, the smashed billboard, the gun. I was aching, bleeding, still half-dazed. I expected to hear police sirens at any moment—all the more reason I should kill myself first.

I staggered up the porch steps. I found the key we kept hidden under a phony rock in a flower box (my sister's idea). Looking over both shoulders, seeing nothing—no police, no people, not a single car coming from either direction—I pushed the door open and went inside.

പ THE HOUSE WAS musty, and there was a faint, sweet smell of carpet cleaner, as if someone (the caretaker we paid?) had recently shampooed it. I stepped past the hallway closet and the banister we used to slide down as kids. I entered the kitchen, with its old tile floor and its cherrywood cabinets. I opened the refrigerator because I was looking for something alcoholic; by now this was a reflex with me.

And I stepped back.

There was food inside.

Tupperware. Leftover lasagna. Skim milk. Apple juice.

Raspberry yogurt. For a fleeting moment, I wondered if someone had moved in, a squatter of some kind, and this was now his place, the price we paid for ignoring it for so long.

I opened a cabinet. There was Lipton tea and a bottle of Sanka. I opened another cabinet. Sugar. Morton salt. Paprika. Oregano. I saw a dish in the sink, soaking under bubbles. I lifted it and slowly lowered it, as if trying to put it back in place.

And then I heard something.

It came from upstairs.

"Charley?"

Again.

"Charley?"

It was my mother's voice.

I ran out the kitchen door, my fingers wet with soapy water.

Times I Did *Not* Stand Up for My Mother

I am six years old. It is Halloween. The school is having its annual Halloween parade. All the kids will march a few blocks through the neighborhood.

"Just buy him a costume," my father says. "They have 'em at the five-and-dime."

But no, my mother decides, since this is my first parade, she will make *me a costume: the mummy, my favorite scary character.*

She cuts up white rags and old towels and wraps them around me, holding them in place with safety pins. Then she layers the rags with toilet paper and tape. It takes a long time, but when she is finished, I look in the mirror. I am a mummy. I lift my shoulders and sway back and forth.

"Oooh, you're very scary," my mother says.

She drives me to school. We start our parade. The more I walk, the looser the rags get. Then, about two blocks out, it begins to rain. Next thing I know, the toilet paper is dissolving. The rags droop. Soon they fall to my ankles, wrists, and neck, and you can see my undershirt and pajama bottoms, which my mother thought would make better undergarments.

"Look at Charley!" the other kids squeal. They are

laughing. I am burning red. I want to disappear, but where do you go in the middle of a parade?

When we reach the schoolyard, where the parents are waiting with cameras, I am a wet, sagging mess of rags and toilet paper fragments. I see my mother first. As she spots me, she raises her hand to her mouth. I burst into tears.

"You ruined my life!" I yell.

"*C*HARLEY?"

What I remember most, hiding on that back porch, is how fast my breath left me. One second I had been at the refrigerator, dragging through the motions, the next second my heart was racing so fast I thought no amount of oxygen could sustain it. I was shaking. The kitchen window was at my back, but I didn't dare look through it. I had seen my dead mother, and now I had heard her voice. I had broken parts of my body before, but this was the first time I worried I had damaged my mind.

I stood there, my lungs heaving in and out, my eyes locked on the earth in front of me. As kids, we'd called this our "backyard," but it was just a square of grass. I thought about bounding across it to a neighbor's house.

And then the door opened.

And my mother stepped outside.

My mother.

Right there. On that porch.

And she turned to me.

And she said, "What are you doing out here? It's cold."

———

NOW, I DON'T know if I can explain the leap I made. It's like jumping off the planet. There is everything you know and there is everything that happens. When the two do not line up, you make a choice. I saw my mother, alive, in front of me. I heard her say my name again. "Charley?" She was the only one who ever called me that.

Was I hallucinating? Should I move toward her? Was she like a bubble that would burst? Honestly, at this point, my limbs seemed to belong to someone else.

"Charley? What's the matter? You're all cut."

She was wearing blue slacks and a white sweater now—she was always dressed, it seemed, no matter how early in the morning—and she looked to be no older than the last time I had seen her, on her seventy-ninth birthday, wearing these red-rimmed glasses she got as a present. She turned her palms gently upward and she beckoned me with her eyes and, I don't know, those glasses, her skin, her hair, her opening the back door the way she used to when I threw tennis balls off the roof of our house. Something melted inside of me, as if her face gave off heat. It went down my back. It went to my ankles. And then something broke, I almost heard the snap, the barrier between belief and disbelief.

I gave in.

Off the planet.

"Charley?" she said. "What's wrong?"

I did what you would have done.

I hugged my mother as if I'd never let her go.

Times My Mother Stood Up for Me

I am eight years old. I have a homework assignment. I must recite to the class: "What Causes an Echo?"

At the liquor store after school, I ask my father. What causes an echo? He is bent over in the aisle, checking inventory with a clipboard and a pencil.

"I don't know, Chick. It's like a ricochet."

"Doesn't it happen in mountains?"

"Mmm?" he says, counting bottles.

"Weren't you in mountains in the war?"

He shoots me a look. "What're you asking about that for?"

He returns to his clipboard.

That night, I ask my mother. What causes an echo? She gets the dictionary, and we sit in the den.

"Let him do it himself," my father snaps.

"Len," she says, "I'm allowed to help him."

For an hour, she works with me. I memorize the lines. I practice by standing in front of her.

"What causes an echo?" she begins.

"The persistence of sound after the source has stopped," I say.

"What is one thing required for an echo?"

"The sound must bounce off something."

"When can you hear an echo?"

"When it's quiet and other sounds are absorbed."

She smiles. "Good." Then she says, "Echo," and covers her mouth and mumbles, "Echo, echo, echo."

My sister, who has been watching our performance, points and yells, "That's Mommy talking! I see her!"

My father turns on the TV set.

"What a colossal waste of time," he says.

The Melody Changes

DO YOU REMEMBER THAT SONG, "This Could Be the Start of Something Big?" It was a fast, upbeat tune, usually sung by a guy in a tuxedo in front of a big band. It went like this:

> *You're walkin' along the street, or you're at a party,*
> *Or else you're alone and then you suddenly dig,*
> *You're lookin' in someone's eyes, you suddenly realize*
> *That this could be the start of something big.*

My mother loved that song. Don't ask me why. They played it at the start of *The Steve Allen Show* back in the 50s, which I recall as a black-and-white program, although everything seemed to be in black and white in those days. Anyhow, my mother thought that song was "a swinger," that's what she called it—"Oooh, that one's a *swinger*!"—and whenever it came on the radio, she snapped her fingers like she was leading the band. We had a hi-fi, and one year for her birthday she got an album by Bobby Darin. He sang that tune, and she played the record after dinner as she cleaned the dishes. This was when my dad was still in the picture. He'd be reading his newspaper and she would walk over to him and drum on his shoulders, singing "this could be the start of something big," and, of course, he wouldn't even look up. Then she'd come over to me and make like she was playing drumsticks on my chest as she sang along.

You're dining at Twenty-One and watching your diet,
Declining a charlotte rousse, accepting a fig,
Then out of the clear blue sky, it's suddenly gal and guy,
And this could be the start of something big.

I wanted to laugh—especially when she said "fig"—but since my father wasn't participating, laughter felt like a betrayal. Then my mother started tickling me and I couldn't help it.

"This could be the start of something big," she'd say, "big boy, big boy, bigboybigboybigboy."

She used to play that music every night. But once my father left, she never did again. The Bobby Darin album stayed on the shelf. The record player collected dust. At first I thought she had changed her taste in music, the way we did as kids, at one point thinking Johnnie Ray was a good singer, but eventually thinking Gene Vincent was so much better. Later, I figured she didn't want to be reminded of how the "something big" had backfired.

The Encounter Inside the House

OUR KITCHEN TABLE WAS ROUND and made of oak. One afternoon when we were in grade school, my sister and I carved our names in it with steak knives. We hadn't finished when we heard the door open—our mother was home from work—so we threw the steak knives back in the drawer. My sister grabbed the biggest thing she could find, a half gallon of apple juice, and plopped it down. When my mother entered, wearing her nurse's outfit, her arms full of magazines, we must have said, "Hi, Mom" too quickly, because she immediately became suspicious. You can see that in your mother's face right away, that "What did you kids do?" look. Maybe because we were sitting at an otherwise empty table at 5:30 in the afternoon with a half gallon of apple juice between us.

Anyhow, without letting go of her magazines, she nudged the juice aside and saw CHAR and ROBER—which was as far as we got—and she let out a loud, exasperated sound, something like "uhhhhch." Then she screamed, "Great, just great!" and in my childish mind, I thought maybe it wasn't so bad. Great was great, right?

My father was traveling in those days, and my mother threatened his wrath when he got home. But that night as we sat at the table eating a meat loaf with a hard-boiled egg inside it—a recipe she had read somewhere, perhaps in one of those magazines she carried—my sister and I kept glancing at our work.

"You know you've completely ruined this table," my mother said.

"Sorry," we mumbled.

"And you could have cut your fingers off with those knives."

We sat there, admonished, lowering our heads to the obligatory level for penance. But we were both thinking the same thing. Only my sister said it.

"Should we finish, so at least we spell our names right?"

I stopped breathing for a moment, astonished at her courage. My mother shot her a dagger-like stare. Then she burst out laughing. And my sister burst out laughing. And I spit out a mouthful of meatloaf.

We never finished the names. They remained there always as CHAR and ROBER. My father, of course, blew a gasket when he got home. But I think over the years, long after we'd departed Pepperville Beach, my mother came to like the idea that we had left something behind, even if we were a few letters short.

NOW I SAT at that old kitchen table, and I saw those markings, and then my mother—or her ghost, or whatever she was—came in from the other room with an antiseptic bottle and a washcloth. I watched her pour the antiseptic into the fabric, then reach for my arm and push up my shirtsleeve, as if I were a little boy who had fallen off the swing set. Perhaps you're thinking: Why not scream out the absurdity of the situation, the obvious facts that made this all impossible, the first of which is, "Mother, you died"?

I can only answer by saying it makes sense to me now as it makes sense to you now, in the retelling, but not in that moment. In that moment, I was so stunned by seeing my mother again that correcting it seemed impossible. It was dream-like, and maybe part of me felt I was dreaming, I don't know. If you've lost your mother, can you imagine seeing her right in front of you again, close enough to touch, to smell? I knew we had buried her. I remembered the funeral. I remembered shoveling a symbolic pile of dirt on her coffin.

But when she sat down across from me and dabbed the washcloth on my face and arms, and she grimaced at the cuts and mumbled, "Look at you"—I don't know how to say it. It burst through my defenses. It had been a long time since anyone wanted to be that close to me, to show the tenderness it took to roll up a shirtsleeve. She cared. She gave a crap. When I lacked even the self-respect to keep myself alive, she dabbed my cuts and I fell back into being a son; I fell as easily as you fall into your pillow at night. And I didn't want it to end. That's the best way I can explain it. I knew it was impossible. But I didn't want it to end.

"Mom?" I whispered.

I hadn't said it in so long. When death takes your mother, it steals that word forever.

"Mom?"

It's just a sound really, a hum interrupted by open lips. But there are a zillion words on this planet, and not one of them comes out of your mouth the way that one does.

"Mom?"

She wiped my arm gently with the washcloth.

"Charley." She sighed. "The trouble you get into."

Times My Mother Stood Up for Me

I am nine years old. I am at the local library. The woman behind the desk looks over her glasses. I have chosen 20,000 Leagues Under the Sea *by Jules Verne. I like the drawings on the cover and I like the idea of people living under the ocean. I haven't looked at how big the words are, or how narrow the print. The librarian studies me. My shirt is untucked and one shoe is untied.*

"This is too hard for you," *she says.*

I watch her put it on a shelf behind her. It might as well be locked in a vault. I go back to the children's section and choose a picture book about a monkey. I return to the desk. She stamps this one without comment.

When my mother drives up, I scramble into the front seat of her car. She sees the book I've chosen.

"Haven't you read that one already?" *she asks.*

"The lady wouldn't let me take the one I wanted."

"What lady?"

"The librarian lady."

She turns off the ignition.

"Why wouldn't she let you take it?"

"She said it was too hard."

"What was too hard?"

"The book."

My mother yanks me from the car. She marches me through the door and up to the desk.

"I'm Mrs. Benetto. This is my son, Charley. Did you tell him a book was too hard for him to read?"

The librarian stiffens. She is much older than my mother, and I am surprised at my mother's tone, given how she usually talks to old people.

"He wanted to take out 20,000 Leagues Under the Sea *by Jules Verne," she says, touching her glasses. "He's too young. Look at him."*

I lower my head. Look at me.

"Where's the book?" my mother says.

"I beg your pardon?"

"Where's the book?"

The woman reaches behind her. She plops it on the counter, as if to make a point by its heft.

My mother grabs the book and shoves it in my arms.

"Don't you ever *tell a child something's too hard," she snaps. "And never—NEVER—this child."*

Next thing I know I am being yanked out the door, hanging tightly to Jules Verne. I feel like we have just robbed a bank, my mother and me, and I wonder if we're going to get in trouble.

Times I Did *Not* Stand Up for My Mother

We are at the table. My mother is serving dinner. Baked ziti with meat sauce.

"It's still not right," my father says.

"Not again," my mother says.

"Not again," my little sister mimics. She rolls her fork in her mouth.

"Watch, you'll stick yourself," my mother says, pulling my sister's hand away.

"It's something with the cheese, or the oil," my father says, looking at his food as if it disgusts him.

"I've tried ten different ways," my mother says.

"Don't exaggerate, Posey. Is it such a big deal to make something I can eat?"

"You can't eat it? It's inedible now?"

"Jesus," he groans. "Do I need this?"

My mother stops looking at him.

"No, you don't need it," she says, scooping a portion angrily onto my plate. "But I need it, right? I need an argument. Eat, Charley."

"Not so much," I say.

"Eat what I give you," she snaps.

"It's too much!"

"*Mommy,*" my sister says.

"*All I'm saying, Posey, is if I ask you to do it, you can do it. That's all. I told you a million times why it don't taste right. If it ain't right, it ain't right. You want me to lie to make you happy?*"

"*Mommy,*" my sister says. She is waving her fork.

"*Acchh,*" my mother gasps, lowering my sister's fork. "*Stop that, Roberta. You know what, Len? Make it yourself next time. You and this whole Italian cooking thing. Charley, eat!*"

My father sneers and shakes his head. "*Same old story,*" he grouses. I am watching him. He sees me. I quickly put a forkful in my mouth. He motions with his chin.

"*What do you think of the ziti your mother made?*" he says.

I chew. I swallow. I look at him. I look at my mother. She drops her shoulders in exasperation. Now they are both waiting.

"*It's not right,*" I mumble, looking at my father.

He snorts and shoots my mother a look.

"*Even the kid knows,*" he says.

A Fresh Start

"So can you stay all day?" my mother asked.

She was standing over the range, scrambling eggs with a plastic spatula. Toast had already been popped, and a stick of butter sat on the table. A pot of coffee was alongside it. I slumped there, still dazed, having trouble even swallowing. I felt that if I moved too quickly, everything would burst. She had tied an apron around her waist and had acted, in the minutes since I first saw her, as if this were just another day, as if I had surprised her with a visit, and in return, she was cooking me breakfast.

"Can you, Charley?" she said. "Spend a day with your mother?"

I heard the sizzling of butter and eggs.

"Hmm?" she said.

She lifted the fry pan and approached.

"Why so quiet?"

It took a few seconds to find my voice, as if I were remembering instructions on how to do it. How do you talk to the dead? Is there another set of words? A secret code?

"Mom," I finally whispered. "This is impossible."

She scooped the eggs from the pan and chop-chop-chopped them on my plate. I watched her veined hands work the spatula.

"Eat," she said.

AT SOME POINT in American history, things must have changed, and divorcing parents informed their children as a team. Sat them down. Explained the new rules. My family collapsed before that age of enlightenment; when my father was gone, he was gone.

After a few weepy days, my mother put on lipstick, did her eyes with mascara, cooked up some fried potatoes, and said, as she handed us our plates, "Dad isn't going to live here anymore." And that was that. It was like a set change in a play.

I can't even remember when he got his stuff. One day we came home from school and the house just seemed more roomy. There was extra space in the front hall closet. The garage was missing tools and boxes. I remember my sister crying and asking, "Did I make Daddy go away?" and promising my mother that she would behave better if he came home. I remember wanting to cry myself, but it had already dawned on me that there were now three of us, not four, and I was the only male. Even at eleven, I felt an obligation to manhood.

Besides, my father used to tell me to "buck up" whenever I cried. "Buck up, kid, buck up." And, like all children whose parents split, I was trying to behave in a way that would bring the missing one back. So no tears, Chick. Not for you.

℺ FOR THE FIRST few months, we figured it was temporary. A spat. A cooling-off period. Parents fight, right? Ours did. My sister and I would lie at the top of the staircase listening to their arguments, me in my white undershirt and she in her pale yellow pajamas and ballerina slippers. Sometimes they argued about us:

"Why don't you handle it for once, Len?"

"It's not that big a deal."

"Yes it is! And I'm always the witch who has to tell them!"

Or about work:

"You could pay more attention, Posey! Those people at the hospital aren't the only ones who matter!"

"They're sick, Len. You want me to tell them I'm sorry, but my husband needs his shirts ironed?"

Or about my baseball:

"It's too much, Len!"

"He could make something of himself."

"Look at him! He's exhausted all the time!"

Sometimes, sitting on those steps, my sister would put her hands over her ears and cry. But I tried to listen. It was like sneaking into a grown-up world. I knew my father worked late and in the last few years, he'd gone on overnight trips to his liquor distributors, telling my mother, "Posey, if you don't schmooze these guys, they gut you like a fish." I knew that he was setting up another store in Collingswood, about an hour away, and he worked there a few days a week. I knew a new store would mean "more money and a better car." I knew my mother didn't like the whole idea.

So, yes, they fought, but I never imagined consequences. Parents didn't split up back then. They worked it out. They stayed on the team.

I remember a wedding once when my father rented a tuxedo and my mother wore a shiny red dress. During the reception, they got up to dance. I saw my mother lift her right hand. I saw my father put his big mitt alongside it. And as young as I was, I could tell they were the best-looking people on the floor. My father cut a tall, athletic figure, and, unlike other fathers, his belly was flat behind his ribbed white shirt. And my mother? Well, she looked happy, smiling with her creamy red lipstick. And when she looked happy, everyone took a backseat. She was such a smooth dancer, you couldn't help but watch her, and her shiny dress seemed spotlighted as she moved. I heard some older women at the table mumbling "it's a bit much" and "show some modesty," but I could tell they were just jealous because they didn't look as pretty as she did.

So that's how I saw my parents. They fought, but they danced. After my father disappeared, I would think about that wedding constantly. I would almost convince myself he was coming back to see my mother in that red dress. How could he not? But in time I stopped thinking that. In time I came to view that event the way you view a faded vacation photo. It's just someplace you went a long time ago.

"What do you want to do this year?" my mother asked me the first September after they got divorced. School was about to start, and she was talking about "new beginnings" and "new projects." My sister had chosen a puppet theater.

I looked at my mother and made the first of a million scowling faces.

"I want to play baseball," I said.

A Meal Together

I DON'T KNOW how much time passed in that kitchen—
I still had a spinning, groggy feeling, like when you bang
your head on the trunk of a car—but at some point, maybe
when my mother said, "Eat," I physically surrendered to the
idea of being there. I did what my mother told me.

I put a forkful of eggs into my mouth.

My tongue practically sprung to attention. I hadn't eaten
in two days, and I began shoveling food like a prisoner. The
chewing took my mind off the impossibility of my situation.
And can I be honest? It was as delicious as it was familiar. I
don't know what it is about food your mother makes for you,
especially when it's something that anyone can make—
pancakes, meat loaf, tuna salad—but it carries a certain taste
of memory. My mother used to put chives in her scrambled
eggs—"the little green things" I called them—and here they
were again.

So now I was eating a past-tense breakfast at a past-tense
table with a past-tense mother.

"Slow down, don't make yourself sick," she said.

That, too, was past tense.

When I finished, she took the plates to the sink and ran
water over them.

"Thank you," I mumbled.

She looked up. "Did you just say 'thank you,' Charley?"

I barely nodded.

"For what?"

I cleared my throat. "For breakfast?"

She smiled as she finished scrubbing. I watched her at the sink and had a sudden rush of familiarity, me at this table, her at the dishes. We'd had so many conversations from just this position, about school, about my friends, about what gossip I shouldn't believe from the neighbors, always the rushing sink water causing us to raise our voices.

"You can't be here . . . ," I began. Then I stopped. I couldn't get beyond that sentence.

She shut the faucet and wiped her hands on a towel.

"Look at the time," she said. "We have to get going."

She leaned over and cupped my face. Her fingers were warm and damp from the sink water.

"You're welcome," she said, "for breakfast."

She grabbed her handbag from the chair.

"Now, be a good boy and get your coat on."

July 20, 1959

Dear Charley—

I know you are scared but there is nothing to be scared about. We have all had our tonsils out and look at us. We're OK!

You hold onto this letter. Put it under your pillow before the doctors come in. They're going to give you something to make you sleepy and just before you fall asleep you can remember my letter is there and if you wake up before I get to your room, then you can reach under the pillow and read this again. Reading is like talking, so picture me talking to you there.

And soon I will be.

And then you can have all the ice cream you want! How about that?

I love you every day.

Mom

Chick's Family After the Divorce

*F*OR A WHILE AFTER my parents split up, we tried to stay the same. But the neighborhood wouldn't allow it. Small towns are like metronomes; with the slightest flick, the beat changes. People were nicer to my sister and me. There'd be an extra lollipop at the doctor's office or a larger scoop on the ice cream cone. Older women, encountering us on the street, would squeeze our shoulders earnestly and ask, "*How* are you kids doing?" which struck us as an adult question. The kids' version began with "What."

But if we were showed more kindness, my mother was not. People didn't get divorced back then. I didn't know a single kid who had endured it. Splitting up, at least where we lived, meant something scandalous, and one of the parties would be assigned the blame.

It fell on my mother, mostly because she was still around. Nobody knew what happened between Len and Posey, but Len was gone and Posey was there to be judged. It didn't help that she refused to seek pity or to cry on their shoulders. And, to make matters worse, she was still young and pretty. So to women she was a threat, to men an opportunity, and to kids an oddity. Not really great choices, when you think about it.

Over time, I noticed people looking at my mother differently when we pushed a cart through the local grocery store or when, in that first year after the divorce, she'd drop my sister and me at school in her white nurse's outfit and her white shoes and white hose. She always got out to kiss us good-bye, and I was acutely aware of the other mothers staring. Roberta and I became self-conscious, approaching the school door as if we squeaked.

"Give your mother a kiss," she said one day, leaning over.

"Don't," I said this time, sliding away.

"Don't what?"

"Just . . ." I scrunched my shoulders and winced. "Just don't."

I couldn't look at her, so I looked at my feet. She held there for a moment before straightening. I heard her sniff. I felt her rub my hair.

By the time I looked up, the car was pulling away.

○ ONE AFTERNOON I was playing catch with a friend in the church parking lot when two nuns opened the back door. My friend and I froze, figuring we had done something wrong. But the nuns motioned me over. They each held an aluminum tray. As I approached, I could smell meat loaf and green beans.

"Here," one of them said. "For your family."

I couldn't understand why they were giving me food. But

it wasn't like you said "no thanks" to a nun. So I took the trays and I walked them home, figuring my mother must have ordered them special.

"What's that?" she asked, when I entered the house.

"The nuns gave it to me."

She pulled back the wax paper. She sniffed.

"Did you ask for this?"

"Nuh-uh. I was playing catch."

"You didn't ask for this?"

"No."

"Because we don't need food, Charley. We don't need handouts, if that's what you think."

I got defensive. I didn't really understand "handout," but I could tell it meant something that didn't get handed out to everyone.

"I didn't ask for it!" I protested. "I don't even *like* green beans!"

We looked at each other.

"It's not my *fault*," I said.

She relieved me of the trays and dumped them in the sink. She mashed the meat loaf into the garbage disposal with a large spoon. She did the same with the green beans. She moved so feverishly I couldn't take my eyes off of her, pounding all that food down that small round hole. She turned on the water. The disposal roared. When the sound pitched higher, meaning it was done, she removed the magnetized top. She shut off the water. She wiped her hands on the front of her apron.

"So," she said, turning to me, "are you hungry?"

☙ THE FIRST TIME I heard the word "divorcée" was after an American Legion baseball game. The coaches were throwing bats in the back of a station wagon, and one of the fathers from the other team picked up my bat by mistake. I ran over and said, "That one's mine."

"It is?" he said, rolling it in his palm.

"Yeah. I brought it with me on my bike."

He could have doubted that, since most kids came with their dads.

"OK," he said, handing it over. Then he squinted and said, "You're the divorcée's kid, right?"

I looked back, wordless. *Divorcée?* It sounded exotic, and I did not think of my mother that way. The men used to ask, "You're Len Benetto's kid, right?" and I'm not sure which bothered me more, being the son of this new word, or no longer being the son of the old ones.

"So how's your mom doing?" he asked.

I shrugged. "She's doing good."

"Yeah?" he said. His eyes darted around the field, then back to me. "She need any help around the house?"

I felt as if my mother was standing behind me, and I was the only thing between them.

"She's doing good," I said again.

He nodded.

If it's possible to distrust a nod, I did.

෨෭ STILL, IF THAT was the day "divorcée" became familiar, I remember distinctly the day it became abhorrent. My mother had come home from work and sent me to the local market for some ketchup and rolls. I decided to take a shortcut through the backyards. When I came around the side of a brick ranch house, I saw two older kids from school huddled there, one of them, a beefy kid named Leon, shielding something against his chest.

"Hey, Benetto," he said quickly.

"Hey, Leon," I said.

I looked at the other kid. "Hey, Luke."

"Hey, Chick."

"Where you going?" Leon said.

"Fanelli's," I said.

"Yeah?"

"Yeah."

He released his grip. He was holding binoculars.

"What are those for?" I said.

He turned to face the trees. "Army gear," he said. "Bino's."

"Twenty times magnification," Luke said.

"Lemme see."

He handed them over, and I held them to my eyes. They

were warm around the rims. I moved them up and down, catching blurry colors of the sky, then the pine trees, then my feet.

"They use 'em in the war," Luke said, "to locate the enemy."

"They're my dad's," Leon said.

I hated hearing that word. I handed them back.

"See ya," I said.

Leon nodded.

"See ya."

I walked on, but my thoughts were uneasy. Something about how Leon had turned to the trees, too quickly, you know? So I circled back behind the house and hid in the hedges. What I saw bothers me to this day.

The two of them were huddled close now, no longer facing the trees but facing the other way, toward my house, passing the binoculars. I followed the sight line to my mother's bedroom window. I saw her shadow move across the pane, her arms lifted over her head, and I immediately thought: *home from work, changing her clothes, bedroom.* I felt myself go cold. Something shot from my neck to my feet.

"Oooweee," Leon cooed, "look at the *divorcée* . . ."

I don't think I ever felt fury like that, not before and not since. I ran to those boys with blood in my eyes, and even though they were bigger than me, I jumped them from behind and grabbed Leon by the neck and threw punches at anything that moved, anything at all.

Walking

MY MOTHER PULLED ON her white tweed coat and shook her shoulders beneath it, letting it settle. She had spent her final years doing hair and makeup for homebound elderly women, going house to house, keeping their beauty rituals alive. She had three such "appointments" today, she said. I followed her, still dazed, out through the garage.

"Do you want to walk by the lake, Charley?" she said. "It's so nice this time of day."

I nodded speechlessly. How much time had passed since I lay in that wet grass, staring at a wreck? How long before someone tracked me down? I could still taste blood in my mouth, and sharp pain came over me in waves; one minute I was neutral, the next minute everything ached. But here I was, walking down my old block, carrying my mother's purple vinyl bag of hair supplies.

"Mom," I finally mumbled. "How . . . ?"

"How what, honey?"

I cleared my throat.

"How can you *be* here?"

"I live here," she said.

I shook my head.

"Not anymore," I whispered.

She looked up at the sky.

"You know, the day you were born, the weather was like this. Chilly but nice. It was late afternoon when I went into labor, remember?" (As if I should answer, "Oh, yeah, I remember.") "That doctor. What was his name? Rapposo? Dr. Rapposo. He told me I had to deliver by six o'clock because his wife was making his favorite supper, and he didn't want to miss it."

I had heard this story before.

"Fish sticks," I mumbled.

"Fish sticks. Can you imagine? Such an easy thing to make. You'd think if he was rushing so much, it would at least be a steak. Ah, well, I didn't care. He got his fish sticks."

She looked at me playfully.

"And I got you."

We took a few more steps. My forehead pounded. I rubbed it with the ball of my hand.

"What happened, Charley? Are you in pain?"

The question was so simple, it was impossible to answer. Pain? Where should I begin? The accident? The leap? The three-day bender? The wedding? My marriage? The depression? The last eight years? When was I *not* in pain?

"I haven't been so good, Mom," I said.

She kept on walking, inspecting the grass.

"You know, for three years after I married your father, I

wished for a child. In those days, three years to get pregnant, that was a long time. People thought there was something wrong with me. So did I."

She exhaled softly. "I couldn't imagine a life without children. Once, I even . . . Wait. Let's see."

She guided me toward the large tree on the corner near our house.

"This was late one night, when I couldn't sleep." She rubbed her hand over the bark as if unearthing an old treasure. "Ah. Still there."

I leaned in. The word PLEASE had been carved into the side. Small crooked letters. You had to look carefully, but there it was. PLEASE.

"You and Roberta weren't the only ones who carved," she said, smiling.

"What is it?"

"A prayer."

"For a child?"

She nodded.

"For me?"

Another nod.

"On a tree?"

"Trees spend all day looking up at God."

I made a face.

"I know." She lifted her hands in surrender. "You're so *corny*, Mom."

She touched the bark again, then made a small *hmm* sound. She seemed to be considering everything that happened since the afternoon I came into the world. I wondered how that sound would change if she knew the whole story.

"So," she said, moving away, "now you know how badly someone wanted you, Charley. Children forget that sometimes. They think of themselves as a burden instead of a wish granted."

She straightened and smoothed her coat. I wanted to cry. A wish granted? How long had it been since anyone referred to me as anything close to that? I should have been grateful. I should have been ashamed of how I'd turned my back on my life. Instead, I wanted a drink. I craved the darkness of a bar, the low-wattage bulbs, the taste of that numbing alcohol as I watched the glass empty, knowing the sooner it got in me, the sooner it would take me away.

I stepped toward her and put my hand on her shoulder; I half expected it to cut right through, like you see in ghost movies. But it didn't. It rested there, and I felt her narrow bones beneath the fabric.

"You died," I blurted out.

A sudden breeze blew leaves off a pile.

"You make too much of things," she said.

ℭℴ POSEY BENETTO WAS a good talker, everybody said so. But, unlike a lot of good talkers, she was also a good listener.

She listened to patients down at the hospital. She listened to neighbors in beach chairs on hot summer days. She loved jokes. She would push a hand into the shoulder of anyone who made her laugh. She was charming. That's how people thought of her: Charming Posey.

Apparently, that was only as long as my father's big hands were wrapped around her. Once she was divorced, freed of his grasp, other women didn't want that charm anywhere near their husbands.

Thus my mother lost all of her friends. She might as well have had the plague. The card games she and my father used to play with neighbors? Finished. The invitations to birthday parties? Done. On the Fourth of July, you could smell charcoal everywhere—yet no one invited us to their cookout. At Christmastime, you would see cars in front of houses and mingling adults visible through the bay windows. But my mother would be in our kitchen, mixing cookie dough.

"Aren't you going to that party?" we'd ask.

"We're having a party right here," she'd say.

She made it seem like her choice. Just the three of us. For a long time, I believed New Year's Eve was a family event, meant for squeezing chocolate syrup on ice cream and tooting noisemakers by a TV set. It surprised me to learn that my teenaged friends used the night for raiding the family liquor cabinet, because their parents were dressed up and gone by eight o'clock.

"You mean you're stuck with your mom on New Year's?" they would ask.

"Yeah," I'd moan.

But it was my charming mother who was stuck.

Times I Did *Not* Stand Up for My Mother

*I have already given up on Santa Claus by the time my old man
leaves, but Roberta is only six, and she does the whole routine:
leaving cookies, writing a note, sneaking to the window, pointing
at stars and asking, "Is that a reindeer?"*

*The first December we are on our own, my mother wants to
do something special. She finds a complete Santa outfit: the red
jacket, red pants, boots, fake beard. On Christmas Eve, she tells
Roberta to go to bed at nine thirty and to not, whatever she
does, be anywhere near the living room at ten o'clock—which, of
course, means Roberta is out of bed at five minutes to ten and
watching like a hawk.*

*I follow behind her, carrying a flashlight. We sit on the
staircase. Suddenly, the room goes dark, and we hear rustling.
My sister gasps. I flick on my flashlight. Roberta whisper-
screams, "No, Chick!" and I flick it off, but then, being that
age, I flick it back on again and catch my mother in her Santa
suit with a pillow sack. She turns and tries to bellow, "Ho! Ho!
Ho! Who's there?" My sister ducks, but for some reason I keep
that light shining on my mother, right in her bearded face, so
she has to shield her eyes with her free hand.*

"Ho! Ho!" she tries again.

Roberta is scrunched up like a bug, peeking over her fists.

She whispers, "Chick, shut it off! You'll scare him away!" But I can only see the absurdity of the situation, how we are going to have to fake everything from now on: fake a full dinner table, fake a female Santa Claus, fake being a family instead of three quarters of a family.

"It's just Mom," I say flatly.

"Ho! Ho! Ho!" my mother says.

"It is not!" Roberta says.

"Yes it is, you twerp. It's Mom. Santa Claus isn't a girl, stupid."

I keep that light on my mother and I see her posture change—her head drops back, her shoulders slump, like a fugitive Santa caught by the cops. Roberta starts crying. I can tell my mother wants to yell at me, but she can't do that and blow her cover, so she stares me down between her stocking cap and her cotton beard, and I feel my father's absence all over the room. Finally, she dumps the pillowcase of small presents onto the floor and walks out the front door without so much as another "ho, ho, ho." My sister runs back to bed, howling with tears. I am left on the stairs with my flashlight, illuminating an empty room and a tree.

Rose

WE CONTINUED WALKING through the old neighborhood. By now I had settled into a foggy acceptance of this—what would you call it?—temporary insanity? I would go with my mother wherever she wanted to go until whatever I had done caught up with me. To be honest, not all of me wanted it to end. When a lost loved one appears before you, it's your brain that fights it, not your heart.

Her first "appointment" lived in a small brick home in the middle of Lehigh Street, just two blocks from our house. There was a metal awning over the porch and a flower box filled with pebbles. The morning air seemed overly crisp now, and the light was strange, making the edges of the scenery too sharply defined, as if drawn in ink. I still had not seen another person, but it was midmorning and most folks would be working.

"Knock," my mother told me.

I knocked.

"She's hard of hearing. Knock louder."

I rapped on the door.

"Knock again."

I pounded.

"Not so hard," she said.

Finally, the door opened. An elderly woman wearing a smock and holding a walker pushed her lips into a confused smile.

"Good *morrr*ning, Rose," my mother sang. "I brought a young man with me."

"Oooh," Rose said. Her voice was so high it was almost birdlike. "Yes, I see."

"You remember my son, Charley?"

"Oooh. Yes. I see."

She stepped back. "Come in. Come in."

Her house was tidy, small, and seemingly frozen in the 1970s. The carpet was royal blue. The couches were covered in plastic. We followed her to the laundry room. Our steps were unnaturally small and slow, marching behind Rose and her walker.

"Having a good day, Rose?" my mother asked.

"Oooh, yes. Now that you're here."

"Do you remember my son, Charley?"

"Oooh, yes. Handsome."

She said this with her back to me.

"And how are your children, Rose?"

"What's that now?"

"Your children?"

"Oooh." She waved her palm. "They check up on me once a week. Like a chore."

I couldn't tell, at that point, who or what Rose was. An apparition? A real person? Her house felt real enough. The heat was turned up, and the smell of toasted bread lingered from breakfast. We entered the laundry room where a chair was positioned by the sink. A radio was playing some big band song.

"Would you turn that off, young man?" Rose said, without turning around. "The radio. Sometimes I have it too loud."

I found the volume knob and clicked it off.

"Terrible, did you hear?" Rose said. "An accident by the highway. They were talking about it on the news."

I froze.

"A car hit a truck and crashed through a big sign. Knocked it right down. Terrible."

I scanned my mother's face, expecting her to turn and demand my confession. *Admit what you did, Charley.*

"Well, Rose, the news is depressing," she said, still unpacking her bag.

"Oooh, yes," Rose said. "So much so."

Wait. They knew? They didn't know? I had a cold flush of dread, as if someone were about to rap on the windows and demand I come out.

Instead, Rose turned her walker, then her knees, then her skinny shoulders in my direction.

"It's nice that you spend a day with your mother," she said. "Children should do it more often."

She put a shaky hand on the back of the chair by the sink.

"Now, Posey," she said, "can you still make me beautiful?"

◈ MAYBE YOU'RE WONDERING how my mother came to be a hairdresser. As I mentioned, she had been a nurse, and she truly loved being a nurse. She had that deep well of patience to carefully dress bandages, draw blood, and answer endless worried questions with upbeat reassurances. The male patients liked having someone young and pretty around. And the female patients were grateful when she brushed out their hair or helped them put on lipstick. I doubt it was protocol back then, but my mother applied makeup to more than a few occupants of our county hospital. She believed it made them feel better. That was the point of a hospital stay, wasn't it? "You're not supposed to go there and rot," she would say.

Sometimes, at the dinner table, she would get a faraway look and talk about "poor Mrs. Halverson" and her emphysema or "poor Roy Endicott" and his diabetes. Now and then, she would stop talking about a person, and my sister would ask, "What did the old lady Golinski do today?" and my mother would answer, "She went home, honey." My father would lift his eyebrows and look at her, then go back to chewing his food. It was only when I got older that I realized "home" meant "dead." That was usually when he changed the subject, anyhow.

෨ THERE WAS ONLY one hospital in our county, and with my father out of the picture, my mother tried to work as many shifts as she could, meaning she couldn't pick up my sister after school. So most days I would fetch Roberta, walk her home, then ride my bike back for baseball practice.

"Do you think Daddy will be there today?" she would ask.

"No, stupid," I would say. "Why would he be there today?"

"Because the grass is high and he has to mow it," she'd say. Or, "Because there are a lot of leaves to rake." Or, "Because it's Thursday, and Mommy makes lamb chops on Thursday."

"I don't think that's a good reason," I'd say.

She'd wait before asking the obvious follow-up.

"Then how come he left, Chick?"

"I dunno! He just did, OK?"

"That's not a good reason, either," she'd mumble.

One afternoon, when I was twelve and she was seven, my sister and I emerged from the schoolyard and heard a honking sound.

"It's Mommy!" Roberta said, running ahead.

She didn't get out of the car, which was strange. My mother thought it rude to honk for people; years later she would warn my sister that any boy who wouldn't come to the front door was a boy not worth dating. But now here she was, staying in the car, so I followed after my sister and crossed the street and got in.

My mother did not look well. Her eyes were black below the lids, and she kept clearing her throat. She was not wearing her nursing whites.

"Why are you here?" I asked. That was how I was talking to her in those days.

"Give your mother a kiss," she said.

I leaned my head across the seat and she kissed my hair.

"Did they let you out of work early?" Roberta asked.

"Yes, sweetie, something like that."

She sniffed. She looked in the rearview mirror and wiped the black from around her eyes.

"How about some ice cream?" she said.

"Yeah! Yeah!" my sister said.

"I have practice," I said.

"Oh, why don't you skip the practice, OK?"

"No!" I protested. "You can't skip practice; you have to go."

"Says who?"

"The coaches and everyone."

"I wanna go! I want a cone!" Roberta said.

"Just a fast ice cream?" my mother said.

"Gaw! No! OK?"

I lifted my head and looked straight at her. What I saw, I don't think I had ever seen before. My mother looked lost.

I would later learn that she had been fired from the hospital. I would later learn that some staff members felt that she was too much of a distraction to the male doctors, now that she was single. I would later learn that there had been some incident with a senior member of the staff and my mother had complained about inappropriate behavior. Her reward for standing up for herself was the suggestion that "it isn't going to work out anymore."

And you know the weird thing? Somehow, I knew all this the moment I looked her in the eye. Not the details, of course. But lost is lost, and I knew that look because I'd worn it myself. I hated her for having it. I hated her for being as weak as I was.

I got out of the car and said, "I don't want any ice cream. I'm going to practice." As I crossed the street, my sister yelled out the window, "Do you want us to bring you a cone?" and I thought, You're so stupid, Roberta, cones melt.

Times I Did *Not* Stand Up for My Mother

She has found my cigarettes. They are in my sock drawer. I am fourteen years old.

"It's my room!" I yell.

"Charley! We talked about this! I told you not to smoke! It's the worst thing you can do! What's the matter with you?"

"You're a hypocrite!"

She stops. Her neck stiffens. "Don't you use that word."

"You smoke! You're a hypocrite!"

"Don't you use that *word!*"

"Why not, Mom? You always want me to use big words in a sentence. There's a sentence. You smoke. I can't. My mother is a hypocrite!"

I am moving as I yell this, and the moving seems to give me strength, confidence, as if she can't hit me. This is after she has taken a job at the beauty parlor, and instead of her nursing whites, she wears fashionable clothes to work—like the pedal pushers and turquoise blouse she is wearing now. These clothes show off her figure. I hate them.

"I am taking these away," she yells, grabbing the cigarettes. "And you are *not* going out, mister!"

"I don't care!" I glare at her. "And why do you have to dress like that? You make me sick!"

"I what?" Now she is on me, slapping my face. "I WHAT? I make you"—slap!—"sick? I make"—slap!—"you SICK?"—slap!—"Is that what you"—slap!—"said?"—slap, slap!—"Is it? Is that what you THINK OF ME?"

"No! No!" I yell. "Stop it!"

I cover my head and duck away. I run down the stairs and out the garage. I stay away until well past dark. When I finally come home, her bedroom door is closed and I think I hear her crying. I go to my room. The cigarettes are still there. I light one up and start crying myself.

Embarrassed Children

Rose had her head tipped back in the sink, and my mother was gently spraying her with water from a faucet attachment. Apparently, they had a whole routine worked out. They propped pillows and towels until Rose's head was just so, and my mother could run her free hand through Rose's wet hair.

"Is that warm enough, hon?" my mother said.

"Oooh, yes, dear. It's fine." Rose closed her eyes. "You know, Charley, your mother has been doing my hair since I was a much younger woman."

"You're young at heart, Rose," my mother said.

"That's the only part."

They laughed.

"When I went to the beauty parlor, I would only ask for Posey. If Posey wasn't there, I would come back the next day. 'Don't you want someone else?' they'd say. But I said, 'Nobody touches me but Posey.'"

"You're sweet, Rose," my mother said. "But the other girls were good."

"Oh, dear, hush. Let me brag. Your mother, Charley, always made time for me. And once it got too hard for me to go to the beauty parlor, she came to my house, every week."

She tapped her shaky fingers on my mother's forearm.

"Thank you, dear, for that."

"You're welcome, Rose."

"Such a beauty you were, too."

I watched my mother smile. How could she be so proud of washing someone's hair in a sink?

"You should see Charley's little girl, Rose," my mother said. "Talk about a beauty. She's a little heartbreaker."

"Is that so? What's her name?"

"Maria. Isn't she a heartbreaker, Charley?"

How could I answer that? The last time they had seen each other was the day my mother died, eight years earlier. Maria was still a teenager. How could I tell her what had happened since? That I had fallen out of my daughter's life? That she had a new last name? That I had sunk so low I had been banished from her wedding? She used to love me, she honestly did. She used to run at me when I came home from work, her arms raised, yelling, "Daddy, pick me up!"

What happened?

"Maria is ashamed of me," I finally mumbled.

"Don't be silly," my mother said.

She looked over at me and rubbed shampoo between her palms. I lowered my head. I wanted a drink in the worst way. I could feel her eyes. I could hear her fingers kneading Rose's hair. Of all the things I felt disgraced about in front of my mother, being a lousy father was the worst.

"You know something, Rose?" she suddenly said. "Charley never let me cut his hair. Can you believe that? He insisted on going to a barbershop."

"Why, dear?"

"Oh, you know. They get to an age and it's 'Get away, Mom, get away.' "

"Children get embarrassed by their parents," Rose said.

"Children get embarrassed by their parents," my mother repeated.

It was true, as a teenager, I had pushed my mother away. I refused to sit next to her at movies. I squirmed from her kisses. I was uncomfortable with her womanly figure and I was angry that she was the only divorced woman around. I wanted her to behave like the other mothers, wearing housedresses, making scrapbooks, baking brownies.

"Sometimes your kids will say the nastiest things, won't they, Rose? You want to ask, 'Whose child *is* this?' "

Rose chuckled.

"But usually, they're just in some kind of pain. They need to work it out."

She shot me a look. "Remember, Charley. Sometimes, kids want you to hurt the way they hurt."

To hurt the way they hurt? Was that what I had done? Had I wanted to see on my mother's face the rejection I felt from my father? Had my daughter done the same to me?

"I didn't mean anything by it, Mom," I whispered.

"By what?"

"Being embarrassed. By you, or your clothes or . . . your situation."

She rinsed the shampoo from her hands, then directed the water to Rose's scalp.

"A child embarrassed by his mother," she said, "is just a child who hasn't lived long enough."

℘ THERE WAS A cuckoo clock in the den, and it broke the silence with small chimes and a mechanical sliding noise. My mother was trimming Rose's hair now with a comb and scissors.

The phone rang.

"Charley, dear," Rose said. "Could you get that for me?"

I walked into the next room, following the ring until I saw a phone hanging on the wall outside the kitchen.

"Hello?" I said into the receiver.

And everything changed.

"CHARLES BENETTO?"

It was a man's voice screaming.

"CHARLES BENETTO! CAN YOU HEAR ME, CHARLES?"

I froze.

"CHARLES? I KNOW YOU CAN HEAR ME! CHARLES! THERE'S BEEN AN ACCIDENT! TALK TO US!"

Hands shaking, I placed the phone back in the cradle.

Times My Mother Stood Up for Me

It is three years after my father's departure. In the middle of the night, I awaken to the sound of my sister thumping down the hall. She is always running to my mother's bedroom. I bury my head in the pillow, drifting back to sleep.

"Charley!" My mother is suddenly in my room, whispering loudly. "Charley! Where's your baseball bat?"

"Wha?" I grunt, rising to my elbows.

"Shhh!" my sister says.

"A bat," my mother says.

"Why do you want a bat?"

"Shhh!" my sister says.

"She heard something."

"A robber's in the house?"

"Shhh!" my sister says.

My heart races. As kids, we have heard of cat burglars (although we think they steal cats) and we have heard of thieves who break into houses and tie up the residents. I immediately imagine something worse, an intruder whose sole purpose is to kill us all.

"Charley? The bat?"

I point to the closet. My chest is heaving. She finds my black Louisville Slugger, and my sister lets go of her hand and jumps into my bed. I am pushing my palms into the mattress, not sure what role I should play.

My mother eases out the door. "Stay here," she whispers. I want to tell her that her grip is wrong. But she's gone.

My sister is trembling next to me. I am ashamed to be lumped in with her, so I slide out from the bed to the door frame, despite her pulling at my pajama bottoms so hard they nearly rip.

In the hallway, I hear every creak of the house settling, and in each one I imagine a thief with a knife. I hear what seems to be a soft thudding. I hear footsteps. I imagine a big, ruddy beast of a man coming up the stairs for my sister and me. Then I hear something real, a smash. Then I hear . . . voices? Is it voices? Yes. No. Wait, that's my mother's voice, right? I want to run downstairs. I want to run back to bed. I hear something deeper— is it another voice? A man's voice?

I swallow.

Moments later, I hear a door close. Hard.

Then I hear footsteps approaching.

My mother's voice precedes her. "It's all right, it's all right," she is saying, no longer whispering, and she moves quickly into the room and rubs my head as she passes me to get to my sister. She drops the bat and it clunks on the floor. My sister is crying. "It's all right. It was nothing," my mother says.

I slump against the wall. My mother hugs my sister. She exhales longer than I have ever heard anyone exhale before.

"Who was it?" I ask.

"Nothing, nobody," she says. But I know she is lying. I know who it was.

"Come here, Charley." She holds a hand out. I straggle over, my arms at my side. She pulls me in, but I resist. I am angry with her. I will remain angry with her until the day I leave this house for good. I know who it was. And I am angry that she wouldn't let my father stay.

"ALL RIGHT, ROSE," my mother was saying as I reentered the room, "you're going to look beautiful. Just give it a half hour."

"Who was on the phone, dear?" Rose asked me.

I could barely shake my head. My fingers were trembling.

"Charley?" my mother asked. "Are you all right?"

"It wasn't . . ." I swallowed. "There was no one there."

"Maybe it was a salesman," Rose said. "They're afraid when men answer the phone. They like old ladies like me."

I sat down. I felt suddenly spent, too tired to keep my chin up. What had just happened? Whose voice was that? How did someone know where to find me, yet not come get me? The harder I tried to think, the dizzier I got.

"Are you tired, Charley?" my mother asked.

"Just . . . give me a second."

My eyes drooped shut.

"Sleep," I heard a voice say, but I couldn't tell which of them said it, that's how gone I was.

Times My Mother Stood Up for Me

I am fifteen and, for the first time, I need to shave. There are stray hairs on my chin and straggly hairs above my lip. My mother calls me to the bathroom one night after Roberta is asleep. She has purchased a Gillette Safety Razor, two stainless-steel blades, and a tube of Burma-Shave cream.

"Do you know how to do this?"

"Of course," I say. I have no idea how to do it.

"Go ahead," she says.

I squeeze the cream from the tube. I dab it on my face.

"You rub it in," she says.

I rub it in. I keep going until my cheeks and chin are covered. I take the razor.

"Be careful," she says. "Pull in one direction, not up and down."

"I know," I say, annoyed. I am uncomfortable doing this in front of my mother. It should be my father. She knows it. I know it. Neither one of us says it.

I follow her instructions. I pull in one direction, watching the cream scrape away in a broad line. When I pull the blade over my chin, it sticks and I feel a cut.

"Oooh, Charley, are you all right?"

She reaches for me, then pulls her hands back as if she knows she shouldn't.

"Stop worrying," I say, determined to keep going.

She watches. I continue. I pull down around my jaw and my neck. When I am finished, she puts her cheek in one hand and smiles. She whispers, in a British accent, "By George, you've got it."

That makes me feel good.

"Now wash your face," she says.

Times I Did *Not* Stand Up for My Mother

It is Halloween. I am sixteen now, too old to go trick-or-treating. But my sister wants me to take her out after supper—she is convinced you get better candy when it's dark—so I reluctantly agree, as long as my new girlfriend, Joanie, can come with us. Joanie is a sophomore cheerleader and I am, by this point, a star on the varsity baseball team.

"Let's go far away and get all new *candy," my sister says.*

It is cold outside, and we dig our hands in our pockets as we walk from house to house. Roberta collects her candy in a brown paper shopping bag. I wear my baseball jacket. Joanie wears her cheerleading sweater.

"Trick or treat!" my sister squeals when a door opens.

"Oh, and who are you, dear?" the woman says. She is about my mother's age, I guess, but she has red hair and is wearing a housedress and has badly drawn eyebrows.

"I'm a pirate," Roberta says. "Grrr."

The woman smiles and drops a chocolate bar in my sister's bag as if dropping a penny in a bank. It goes plunk.

"I'm her brother," I say.

"I'm . . . with them," Joanie says.

"And do I know your parents?"

She is about to drop another bar in my sister's bag.

"My mom is Mrs. Benetto," Roberta says.

The woman halts. She pulls the candy back.

"Don't you mean Miss Benetto?" she says.

None of us know what to say. The woman's expression has changed and those drawn eyebrows are straining downward.

"Now you listen to me, sweetie. Tell your mother that my husband doesn't need to see her little fashion show by his shop every day. Tell her to not get any grand ideas, you hear me? No grand ideas."

Joanie looks at me. The back of my neck is burning.

"Can I have that one, too?" Roberta asks, her eyes on the chocolate.

The woman pulls it closer to her chest.

"Come on, Roberta," I mumble, yanking her away.

"Must run in the family," the woman says. "You all want your hands on everything. You tell her what I said! No grand ideas, you hear me?"

We are already halfway across her lawn.

Rose Says Good-Bye

WHEN WE STEPPED OUT of Rose's house, the sun was brighter than before. Rose followed us as far as the porch, where she remained, the aluminum door frame resting against the side of her walker.

"Well, so long, Rose, honey," my mother said.

"Thank you, dear," she said. "I'll see you soon."

"Of course you will."

My mother kissed her on the cheek. I had to admit, she had done a nice job. Rose's hair was shaped and styled and she looked years younger than when we'd arrived.

"You look nice," I said.

"Thank you, Charley. It's a special occasion."

She readjusted her grip on the walker handles.

"What's the occasion?"

"I'm going to see my husband."

I didn't want to ask where, in case, you know, he was in a home or a hospital, so I blurted out, "Oh, yeah? That's nice."

"Yes," she said softly.

My mother pulled at a stray thread on her coat. Then she looked at me and smiled. Rose moved backward, allowing the door to close.

We stepped down carefully, my mother holding my arm. When we reached the sidewalk, she motioned to the left and we turned. The sun was nearly straight above us now.

"How about some lunch, Charley?" she said.

I almost laughed.

"What?" my mother said.

"Nothing. Sure. Lunch." It made as much sense as anything else.

"You feel better now—with a little nap?"

I shrugged. "I guess."

She tapped my hand affectionately.

"She's dying, you know."

"Who? Rose?"

"Um-hmm."

"I don't get it. She seemed fine."

She squinted up at the sun.

"She'll die tonight."

"Tonight?"

"Yes."

"But she said she's going to see her husband."

"She is."

I stopped walking.

"Mom," I said. "How do you know that?"

She smiled.

"I'm helping her get ready."

III. Noon

Chick and College

I WOULD GUESS the day I went to college was one of the happiest of my mother's life. At least it started out that way. The university had offered to pay half my tuition with a baseball scholarship, although, when my mother told her friends, she just said "scholarship," her love of that word eclipsing any possibility that I was admitted to hit the ball, not the books.

I remember the morning we drove up for my freshman year. She'd been awake before sunrise, and there was a full breakfast waiting for me when I stumbled down the stairs: pancakes, bacon, eggs—six people couldn't have finished that much food. Roberta had wanted to come with us, but I said no way—what I meant was, it was bad enough that I had to go with my mother—so she consoled herself with a plateful of syrup-covered French toast. We dropped her at a neighbor's house and began our four-hour trek.

Because, to my mother, this was a big occasion, she wore one of her "outfits"—a purple pantsuit, a scarf, high heels, and sunglasses, and she insisted that I wear a white shirt and a necktie. "You're starting college, not going fishing," she said. Together we would have stood out badly enough in Pepperville Beach, but remember, this was college in the mid-60s, where the less correctly you were dressed, the more you were dressed correctly. So when we finally got to campus and stepped out of our Chevy station wagon, we were surrounded by young women in sandals and peasant skirts, and young men in tank tops and shorts, their hair worn long over their ears. And there we were, a necktie and a purple pantsuit, and I felt, once more, that my mother was shining a ridiculous light on me.

She wanted to know where the library was, and she found someone to give us directions. "Charley, look at all the books," she marveled as we walked around the ground floor. "You could stay in here all four years and never make a dent."

Everywhere we went she kept pointing. "Look! That cubicle—you could study there." And, "Look, that cafeteria table, you could eat there." I tolerated it because I knew she would be leaving soon. But as we walked across the lawn, a good-looking girl—gum-chewing, white lipstick, bangs on her forehead—caught my eye and I caught hers and I flexed my arm muscles and I thought, my first college girl, who knows? And at that very moment my mother said, "Did we pack your toiletry kit?"

How do you answer that? A yes? A no? A "Jesus, Mom!" It's all bad. The girl continued past us and she sort of guffawed, or maybe I just imagined that. Anyhow, we didn't exist in her universe. I watched her sashay over to two bearded guys sprawled under a tree. She kissed one on the lips and she fell in alongside them, and here I was with my mother asking about my toiletry kit.

An hour later, I hoisted my trunk to the stairwell of my dorm. My mother was carrying my two "lucky" baseball bats with which I had led the Pepperville County Conference in home runs.

"Here," I said, holding out my hand, "I'll take the bats."

"I'll go up with you."

"No, it's all right."

"But I want to see your room."

"Mom."

"What?"

"Come on."

"What?"

"You know. Come on."

I couldn't think of anything else that wouldn't hurt her feelings, so I just pushed my hand out farther. Her face sank. I was six inches taller than her now. She handed me the bats. I balanced them atop the trunk.

"Charley," she said. Her voice was softer now, and it sounded different. "Give your mother a kiss."

I put the trunk down with a small thud. I leaned toward her. Just then two older students came bounding down the stairs, feet thumping, voices loud and laughing. I instinctively jerked away from my mother.

"'Scuse please," one of them said as they maneuvered around us.

Once they were gone, I leaned forward, only intending a peck on the cheek, but she threw her arms around my neck and she drew me close. I could smell her perfume, her hair spray, her skin moisturizer, all the assorted potions and lotions she had doused herself with for this special day.

I pulled away, lifted the trunk, and began my climb, leaving my mother in the stairwell of a dormitory, as close as she would ever get to a college education.

The Middle of the Day

"So how is Catherine?"

We were back in her kitchen, having lunch, as she had suggested. Since I'd been on my own, I had eaten most of my meals from barstools or in fast-food outlets. But my mother had always shunned eating away from home. "Why should we pay for bad food?" she would say. After my father left, it became a moot point. We ate at home because we couldn't afford to eat out anymore.

"Charley? Honey?" she repeated. "How's Catherine?"

"She's OK," I lied, not having any idea how Catherine was.

"And this business about Maria being ashamed of you? What does Catherine say about that?"

She carried over a plate with a sandwich—pumpernickel bread, roast beef, tomato, and mustard. She sliced it diagonally. I can't remember the last time I saw a sandwich sliced diagonally.

"Mom," I said, "to be honest . . . Catherine and I split up."

She finished slicing. She seemed to be thinking about something.

"Did you hear what I said?"

"Mmm," she answered, quietly, without looking up. "Yes, Charley. I did."

"It wasn't her. It was me. I haven't been real good for a while, you know? That's why . . ."

What was I going to say? *That's why I tried to kill myself?* She pushed the plate in front of me.

"Mom . . ." My voice cracked. "We buried you. You've been gone for a long time."

I stared at the sandwich, two triangles of bread. "Everything's different now," I whispered.

She reached over and put my cheek in her hand. She grimaced as if a pain were passing through her.

"Things can be fixed," she said.

September 8, 1967

Charley—

How do you like my typing! I've been practicing at work on Henrietta's typewriter. Pretty snazzy!

I know you won't read this until after I have left. But in case I forgot because I was too excited by the whole idea of you being at college, I want to tell you something. I am so proud of you, Charley. You are the first person in our family to go to a university!

Charley, be nice to the people there. Be nice to your teachers. Always call them Mr. and Mrs., even though I hear now that college students call their teachers by their first names. I don't think that's right. And be nice to the girls you go out with. I know you don't want love life advice from me, but even if girls find you handsome, that is not a license to be mean. Be nice.

And also get your sleep. Josie, who comes into the beauty parlor, says her son at college keeps falling asleep during his classes. Don't insult your teachers that way, Charley. Don't fall asleep. It's such a lucky thing you have, to be taught and to be learning and not have to be working in a shop somewhere.

I love you every day.

And now I will miss you every day.

Love,

Mom

When Ghosts Return

I USED TO DREAM about finding my father. I dreamed he moved to the next town over, and one day I would ride my bike to his house and knock on his door and he would tell me it was all just a big mistake. And the two of us would ride home together, me on the front, my dad pedaling hard behind, and my mother would run out the door and burst into happy tears.

It's amazing the fantasies your mind can put together. The truth was, I didn't know where my father lived and I never did find out. I would go by his liquor store after school, but he was never there. His friend Marty was managing it now, and he told me my dad was full-time in the new place in Collingswood. It was only an hour's drive away, but to a kid my age, it might as well have been on the moon. After a while, I stopped going past his store. I stopped fantasizing about us biking home together. I finished grade school, junior high, and high school with no contact from my old man.

He was a ghost.

But I still saw him.

I saw him whenever I swung a bat or threw a ball, which is why I never gave up baseball, why I played through every spring and every summer on every team and in every league possible. I could picture my father at the plate, tipping my elbow, correcting my batting stance. I could hear him yelling, "Dig, dig, dig!" as I ran out a ground ball.

A boy can always see his father on a baseball field. In my mind, it was just a matter of time before he showed up for real.

So, year after year, I pulled on new team uniforms—red socks, gray pants, blue tops, yellow caps—and each one felt like I was dressing for a visit. I split my adolescence between the pulpy smell of books, which was my mother's passion, and the leathery smell of baseball gloves, which was my father's. My body sprouted into his frame, broad and strong-shouldered, but two inches taller.

And as I grew, I held on to the game like a raft in the bumpy sea, faithfully, through the chop.

Until at last, it restored me to my father.

As I always knew it would.

HE REAPPEARED, AFTER an eight-year absence, at my first college game in the spring of 1968, sitting in the front row of seats just left of home plate, from which he could best study my form.

I will never forget that day. It was a windy afternoon and the sky was a gunmetal color, threatening rain. I walked to the plate. I don't usually look at the seats, but for whatever reason, I did. And there he was. His hair was graying at the temples and his shoulders seemed smaller, his waist a bit wider, as if he had sunk down on himself, but otherwise, he looked the same. If he was uncomfortable, he didn't show it. I'm not sure I'd recognize my father's "uncomfortable" look, anyhow.

He nodded at me. Everything seemed to freeze. Eight years. Eight whole years. I felt my lip tremble. I remember a voice in my head saying, *Don't you dare, Chick. Don't you cry, you bastard, don't cry.*

I looked at my feet. I forced them to move. I kept my eyes on them all the way into the batter's box.

And I smacked the first pitch over the left-field wall.

Miss Thelma

*M*Y MOTHER'S NEXT APPOINTMENT, she said, was with someone who lived in a part of town we called the Flats. It was mostly poor people in attached row houses. I was sure we'd need to drive there, but before I could ask, the doorbell rang.

"Answer that, Charley, OK?" my mother said, putting a dish in the sink.

I hesitated. I didn't want to answer any bells or pick up any phones. When my mother called out again, "Charley? Can you get that?" I rose and walked slowly to the door.

I told myself everything was fine. But the instant I touched the knob, I felt a sudden blast that blinded me, a wash of light, and a man's voice, the voice from Rose's telephone. It was screaming now.

"CHARLES BENETTO! LISTEN! I'M A PO-LICE OFFICER!"

It felt like a windstorm. The voice was so close, I could physically touch it.

"CAN YOU HEAR ME, CHARLES? I'M A PO-LICE OFFICER!"

I staggered back and threw my hands over my face. The light disappeared. The wind died. I heard only my own labored breathing. I quickly looked for my mother, but she was still at the sink; whatever I was going through, it was happening in my head.

I waited a few seconds, inhaled three long breaths, then carefully turned the doorknob, eyes lowered, expecting the police officer who'd been screaming at me. I pictured him young for some reason.

But when I lifted my gaze, I saw instead an elderly black woman with spectacles on a chain around her neck, disheveled hair, and a burning cigarette.

"Is that you, Chickadoo?" she said. "Well, look who done grown up."

ᗑᗴ WE CALLED HER Miss Thelma. She used to clean our house. She was lean and narrow-shouldered, with a broad smile and a quick temper. Her hair was dyed a reddish orange and she smoked constantly, Lucky Strikes, which she kept in her shirt pocket, like a man. Born and raised in Alabama, she somehow wound up in Pepperville Beach, where, in the late 1950s, pretty much every house on our side of town employed someone like her. A "domestic" they were called, or, when people were being honest, a "maid." My father would pick her up Saturday mornings at the bus station near the Horn & Hardart cafeteria, and he would pay her before he left the house, slipping her the folded bills low, by her hip, as if neither were supposed to look at the money. She would clean all day while we were out at baseball. By the time we got home, my room was spotless, whether I liked it or not.

My mother insisted we call her "Miss Thelma." I remember that, and I remember we weren't allowed to step into any room she had just vacuumed. I remember she played catch with me sometimes in the backyard, and she could throw as hard as I could.

She also, inadvertently, invented my nickname. My father had tried calling me "Chuck" (my mother hated that, she said, "Chuck? It sounds like a cowhand!"), but because I was always hollering from the yard back into the house, "Mommmm!" or "Roberrrrta!," one day Miss Thelma looked up, annoyed, and said, "Boy, the way you holler, you're like a rooster. Chuckadoodle-doo!" And my sister, who was then a preschooler, said, "Chickadoodle-doo! Chickadoodle-doo!" and, I don't know, somehow, the "Chick" part stuck. I don't think that made my dad too fond of Miss Thelma.

"Posey," she said to my mother now, her grin spreading. "I been thinking about you."

"Well, thank you," my mother said.

"I surely have."

She turned to me.

"Cain't throw you no balls these days, Chickadoo." She laughed. "Too old."

We were in her car, which, I guessed, was how we were getting to the Flats. It seemed odd to me that my mother would do beauty work for Miss Thelma. But then, I knew so little about my mother over the last decade of her life. I had been too wrapped up in my own drama.

As we drove, for the first time, I saw other people out the window. There was a pinched old man with a gray beard carrying a rake to his garage. My mother waved to him and he waved back. There was a woman with hair the color of French vanilla ice cream, wearing a housedress and sitting on her porch. Another wave from my mother. Another wave back.

We drove for a while, until the streets became smaller and rougher. We turned on a gravel road and came to a two-family house with a roofed porch flanked by cellar doors, badly in need of paint. There were several cars parked in the driveway. A bicycle lay on its side in the front yard. Miss Thelma put the car in park and turned the key.

And just like that, we were inside the house. The bedroom was paneled, with olive carpeting. The bed itself was an old four-poster. And Miss Thelma was suddenly lying in it, propped up against two pillows.

"What just happened?" I asked my mother.

She shook her head as if to say, "Not now," and began unpacking her bag. I heard children squealing from another room, and the muffled sounds of a television set and plates being moved around a table.

"They all think I'm sleeping," Miss Thelma whispered. She looked my mother in the eye.

"Posey, I sure would appreciate it now. Could you?"

"Of course," my mother replied.

Times I Did *Not* Stand Up for My Mother

I don't tell her about seeing my father. He shows up for my next game, too, and he nods again when I come to the plate. This time I nod back, barely, but I do. And I go three-for-three in that game, with another home run and two doubles.

We go on like this for several weeks. He sits. He watches. And I hit the ball like it is two feet wide. Finally, after a road game in which I hit two more home runs, he is waiting by the team bus. He wears a blue windbreaker over a white turtleneck. I notice the gray in his sideburns. He lifts his chin when he sees me, as if fighting the fact that I am now taller than him. These are the first words he says:

"Ask your coach if I can drive you back to campus."

I could do anything at this moment. I could spit. I could tell him to go to hell. I could ignore him, the way he ignored us.

I could say something about my mother.

Instead, I do what he asks me to do. I seek permission to skip the bus ride home. He is respecting the authority of my coach, I am respecting the authority of my father, and this is how the world makes sense, all of us behaving like men.

"*I* DON'T KNOW, Posey," Miss Thelma said, "it's gonna take a miracle."

She was looking into a handheld mirror. My mother unloaded small jars and jeweled cases.

"Well, this is my miracle bag," she said.

"Yeah? Y'all got a cure for cancer in there?"

My mother held up a bottle. "I've got moisturizer."

Miss Thelma laughed.

"You think it's silly, Posey?"

"What's that, honey?"

"Wanting to look good—at this point?"

"There's nothing wrong with it, if that's what you mean."

"Well, you see, my boys and girls are out there, that's all. And their little ones. And I wish I could look healthy for them, you know? I don't like to make 'em fret, seeing me look like some old dishrag."

My mother rubbed moisturizer on Miss Thelma's face, making wide circular motions with her palms.

"You could never look like a dishrag," she said.

"Oh, talk to me, Posey."

They laughed again.

"I miss them Saturdays, sometimes," Miss Thelma said. "We had some fun, didn't we?"

"We did at that," my mother said.

"We did at that," Miss Thelma agreed.

She closed her eyes as my mother's hands did their work.

"Chickadoo, your mama is the best partner I ever had."

I wasn't sure what she meant.

"You worked at the beauty parlor?" I said.

My mother grinned.

"Naw," Miss Thelma said. "I couldn't make nobody look better if I tried."

My mother capped the moisturizer bottle and picked up a new jar. She undid the top, and dabbed a small sponge into its contents.

"What?" I said. "I don't get it."

She held up the sponge like an artist about to put brush to canvas.

"We cleaned houses together, Charley," she said.

Upon seeing the look on my face, she waved her fingers dismissively.

"How do you think I put you kids through college?"

BY MY SOPHOMORE YEAR, I'd packed on ten pounds of muscle, and my hitting reflected it. My batting average among college players was in the top fifty in the nation. At my father's urging, I played in several tournaments which were showcases for professional scouts, older men who sat in the stands with notebooks and cigars. One day, one of them approached us after a game.

"This your boy?" he asked my father.

My father nodded suspiciously. The man had thinning hair and a bulbous nose, and his undershirt was visible through his lightweight sweater.

"I'm with the St. Louis Cardinals organization."

"That right?" my father said.

I wanted to leap through my skin.

"We may have a spot at catcher, 'A' ball."

"That right?" my father said.

"We'll keep an eye on your boy, if he's interested."

The man sniffed deeply, a wet, noisy sound. He took out a handkerchief and blew his nose.

"The thing is," my father said, "Pittsburgh has the inside track. They've been scouting him for a while."

The man studied my father's jaw, which worked over the gum he was chewing.

"That right?" the man said.

෨෧ OF COURSE, ALL this was news to me, and when the man departed, I hounded my father with questions. When did this happen? Was that guy for real? Was Pittsburgh really scouting me?

"What if they are?" he said. "It don't change what you gotta do, Chick. You stay in those cages, work with your coaches, and be ready when the time comes. Let me take care of the rest."

I nodded obediently. My mind was racing.

"What about school?"

He scratched his chin. "What about it?"

I flashed on my mother's face, walking me through the library. I tried not to think about it.

"The St. Louis *Caaardinals*," my father drawled, long and slow. He ground his shoe into the grass. Then he actually grinned. I felt so proud I got goose bumps. He asked if I wanted a beer and I said yeah, and we went and had one together, as men do.

෨෧ "DAD CAME TO a game."

I was on the pay phone in the dorm. This was well after my father's first visit, but it had taken me that long to find the courage to tell her.

"Oh," my mother finally said.

"By himself," I quickly added. For some reason, that seemed important.

"Did you tell your sister?"

"No."

Another long silence.

"Don't let anything affect your studying, Charley."

"I won't."

"That's the most important thing."

"I know."

"An education is everything, Charley. An education is how you'll make something of yourself."

I kept waiting for more. I kept waiting for some horrible story about some horrible thing. I kept waiting the way all children of divorce wait, for evidence to tip my scales, a tilt in the floor that made me choose one side over the other. But my mother never spoke about the reason my father left. She never once took the bait Roberta and I dangled before her, looking for hate or bitterness. All she did was swallow. She swallowed the words, she swallowed the conversation. Whatever had happened between them, she swallowed that, too.

"Is it OK that me and Dad see each other?"

"Dad and I," she corrected.

"Dad and I," I said, exasperated. "Is it?"

She exhaled.

"You're not a little boy anymore, Charley."

Why did I feel like one?

⊘⊘ LOOKING BACK ON that now, there is so much I didn't know. I didn't know how she really took that news. I didn't know if it angered her or scared her. I certainly didn't know that while I was having beers with my father, the bills back home were being paid, in part, by my mother cleaning houses with a woman who once cleaned ours.

I watched the two of them now in the bedroom, Miss Thelma upright against the pillows, my mother working her makeup sponges and her eyeliner pencils.

"Why didn't you tell me?" I asked.

"Tell you what?" my mother said.

"That you had to, you know, for money—?"

"Mop floors? Do laundry?" My mother chuckled. "I don't know. Maybe because of the way you're looking at me now."

She sighed. "You were always proud, Charley."

"I was *not*!" I snapped.

She lifted her eyebrows then returned to Miss Thelma's face. Under her breath she mumbled, "If you *say* so."

"Don't do that!" I said.

"Do what?"

"If you *say* so. That."

"I didn't say anything, Charley."

"Yes, you did!"

"Don't yell."

"I wasn't proud! Just because I—"

My voice cracked. What was I doing? A half a day with my dead mother, and we were back to arguing?

"Ain't no shame in needing work, Chickadoo," Miss Thelma said. "But the only work I knew was what I'd been doing. And your mom said, 'Well, what about that?' I said, 'Posey, you want to be somebody's cleaning woman?' And she said, 'Thelma, if you ain't above cleaning a house, why should *I* be?' Remember that, Posey?"

My mother inhaled.

"I didn't say 'ain't.'"

Miss Thelma howled with laughter. "Naw, naw, that's right, you didn't. I'm sure of that. You didn't say 'ain't.'"

They were both laughing now. My mother was trying to work under Miss Thelma's eyes.

"Hold *still*," she said, but they kept on laughing.

"I THINK MOM should get married again," Roberta said.

This was one time when I called home from college.

"What are you talking about?"

"She's still pretty. But nobody stays pretty forever. She's not as thin as she used to be."

"She doesn't want to get married."

"How do you know?"

"She doesn't need to get married, Roberta, OK?"

"If she doesn't get somebody soon, nobody is gonna want her."

"Stop it."

"She wears a girdle now, Charley. I saw it."

"I don't *care*, Roberta! God!"

"You think you're so cool because you go to college."

"Cut it out."

"Did you ever hear that song 'Yummy, Yummy, Yummy'? I think it's so stupid. How come they play it all the time?"

"Is she talking to you about getting married?"

"Maybe."

"Roberta, I'm not kidding. What did she say?"

"Nothing, OK? But who knows where the hell Dad is. And Mom shouldn't have to be by herself all the time."

"Stop cursing," I said.

"I can say whatever I want, Charley. You're not my boss."

She was fifteen. I was twenty. She had no idea about my father. I had seen him and talked to him. She wanted my mother happy. I wanted her to stay the same. It had been nine years since that Saturday morning when my mother crushed the corn puffs in the palm of her hand. Nine years since we'd all been a family.

In college, I had a course in Latin, and one day the word

"divorce" came up. I always figured it came from some root that meant "divide." In truth, it comes from "divertere," which means "to divert."

I believe that. All divorce does is divert you, taking you away from everything you thought you knew and everything you thought you wanted and steering you into all kinds of other stuff, like discussions about your mother's girdle and whether she should marry someone else.

Chick Makes His Choice

*T*HERE ARE TWO DAYS AT COLLEGE that I'll share with you here because they were the high and the low points of that experience. The high came in my second year, sometime during the fall semester. Baseball hadn't started up, so I actually had time to hang out on campus. On a Thursday night after midterm exams, one of the fraternities had a big party. It was crowded and dark. Music blasted. Black lights made the posters on the walls—and everyone at the party—seem phosphorescent. We laughed loudly and toasted each other with plastic cups of beer.

At some point, a guy with long stringy hair jumped on a chair and began lip-synching to the music and playing air guitar—it was a song by the Jefferson Airplane—and it quickly became a contest. We went flipping through the milk crates of albums to find a "performance" song.

Well, I don't know who owned these albums, but I spotted an unlikely one and I yelled to my buddies, "Hey! Wait! Look at this!" It was the Bobby Darin album my mother used to play when we were kids. He wore a white tuxedo on the cover, his hair embarrassingly short and neat.

"I know this one!" I said. "I know all the words!"

"Get out," one buddy said.

"Put it on!" another said. "Look at that dufus!"

We commandeered the turntable, lined up the needle to the groove of "This Could Be the Start of Something Big," and when the music began, everybody froze, because this clearly wasn't rock and roll. Suddenly I was out there with my two pals. They looked at each other, embarrassed, and pointed at me as they shook their hips. But I was feeling loose and I figured, who cares? So as the trumpets and clarinets boomed over the speakers, I mouthed the words that I knew by heart.

"You're walkin' along the street, or you're at a party
Or else you're alone and then you suddenly dig,
You're lookin' in someone's eyes, you suddenly realize
That this could be the start of something big."

I was snapping my fingers like the crooners from *The Steve Allen Show*, and suddenly everyone was laughing and hollering, "Yeah! Go, cat!" I got more and more ridiculous. I guess no one could believe I knew all the words to such a hokey record.

Anyhow, by the time it was done, I got a big ovation and my friends tackled me around the waist, and we pushed into one another, laughing and calling each other names.

I met Catherine that night. This is what makes it the high point. She had watched my "performance" with a few of her girlfriends. I caught sight of her and I shivered—even as I was flapping my arms and lip-synching. She wore a sleeveless pink cotton blouse, hip-hugger jeans and strawberry-colored lip gloss, and she playfully snapped her fingers as I sang Bobby Darin. To this day, I don't know if she would have given me a second look had I not been making such an utter fool of myself.

"Where did you learn that *song*?" she said, stepping up as I drew a beer from the keg.

"Uh...my mom," I answered.

I felt like an idiot. Who begins a conversation with "my mom?" But she seemed to like the idea and, well, we went from there.

The next day I got my grades and they were good, two A's, two B's. I called my mother at the beauty parlor and she came to the phone. I told her the results and I told her about Catherine and the Bobby Darin song and she seemed so happy that I had called her in the middle of the day. Over the rumble of hair dryers she yelled, "Charley, I'm so *proud* of you!"

That was the high point.

I dropped out of college one year later.

That was the low point.

இ I DROPPED OUT to play minor league baseball, at my father's suggestion and to my mother's everlasting disappointment. I had been offered a spot in the Pittsburgh Pirates' organization, to play winter ball and hopefully make their minor league roster. My father felt this was the right time. "You can't get any better playing against college kids," he said.

When I first mentioned the idea to my mother, she screamed, "Absolutely not!" It didn't matter that baseball would pay me. It didn't matter that the scouts thought I had potential—maybe enough to make it to the major leagues. "Absolutely not!" were her words.

And I absolutely ignored her.

I went to the registrar's office, told them I was leaving, packed up a duffel bag, and split. Many guys my age were being sent to Vietnam. But by whatever twist of luck or fate, I had drawn a low number in the draft lottery. My father, a veteran, seemed relieved at that fact. "You don't need the trouble you get into during a war," he said.

Instead, I marched to his cadence, and I followed his command: I joined a minor league club in San Juan, Puerto Rico, and my student days were over. What can I say about that? Was I seduced by baseball or my father's approval? Both, I suppose. It felt natural, like I was back on the trail of breadcrumbs I had followed as a schoolboy—before things flopped over, before my life as a mama's boy had begun.

I remember calling her from the motel phone in San Juan. I had flown there straight from college, the first time I'd ever been on an airplane. I didn't want to stop at home because I knew she would make a scene.

"A collect call from your son," the operator said with a Spanish accent.

When my mother realized where I was, that the deal was done, she seemed stunned. Her voice was flat. She asked what kind of clothes I had. What was I doing for food? She seemed to be reading from a list of required questions.

"Is it safe, the place you're staying?" she said.

"Safe? I guess."

"Who else do you know there?"

"Nobody. But there's guys on the team. I have a roommate. He's from Indiana, or Iowa, someplace."

"Mm-hmm."

Then silence.

"Mom, I can always go back to school."

This time the silence was longer. She said only one more thing before we hung up:

"Going back to something is harder than you think."

I don't suppose I could have broken my mother's heart any more if I tried.

The Work You Have to Do

*M*ISS THELMA CLOSED HER EYES and leaned her head back. My mother resumed her makeup process. She dabbed the sponge around her former partner's face, and I watched with mixed emotions. I always thought it was so important what came after your name. Chick Benetto, *professional baseball player*, not Chick Benetto, *salesman*. Now I'd learned that after Posey Benetto, *nurse*, and Posey Benetto, *beautician*, it was Posey Benetto, *cleaning woman*. It angered me that she had dropped so low.

"Mom . . . ," I said, haltingly. "Why didn't you just get money from Dad?"

My mother set her jaw.

"I didn't need any more from your father."

"Mm-hmm," Miss Thelma added.

"We got by all right, Charley."

"Mm-hmm, you did."

"Why didn't you go back to the hospital?" I said.

"They didn't want me."

"Why didn't you fight it?"

"Would that have made you happy?" She sighed. "It wasn't like today, where people sue over the slightest thing. It was the only hospital around. We couldn't just leave town.

This was our home. You and your sister had endured enough change. It's all right. I found work."

"Cleaning houses," I mumbled.

She put her hands down.

"I'm not as ashamed of that as *you* are," she said.

"But . . ." I stumbled for words. "You couldn't do the work that mattered to you."

My mother looked at me with a glint of defiance.

"I did what mattered to me," she said. "I was a mother."

WE WERE SILENT after that. Finally, Miss Thelma opened her eyes.

"So what about you, Chickadoo?" she said. "You ain't still up on that big stage playing baseball?"

I shook my head.

"Naw, I s'pose not," she said. "Young man's business, baseball is. But you'll always be that little boy to me, with that glove on your hand, so serious and all."

"Charley has a family now," my mother said.

"Is that right?"

"And a good job."

"There you go." Miss Thelma eased her head back. "You're doing awfully fine, then, Chickadoo. Awfully fine."

They were all wrong. I wasn't doing fine.

"I hate my job," I said.

"Well . . ." Miss Thelma shrugged. "Sometimes that happens. Cain't be much worse than scrubbin' your bathtub, can it?" She grinned. "You do what you gotta do to hold your family together. Ain't that right, Posey?"

I watched them finish their routine. I thought about how many years Miss Thelma must have run vacuums or scrubbed tubs to feed her kids; how many shampoos or dye jobs my mother must have done to feed us. And me? I got to play a game for ten years—and I wanted twenty. I felt suddenly ashamed.

"What's wrong with that job you got, anyhow?" Miss Thelma said.

I pictured the sales office, the steel desks, the dim, fluorescent lights.

"I didn't want to be ordinary," I mumbled.

My mother looked up. "What's ordinary, Charley?"

"You know. Someone you forget."

From the other room came the squeals of children. Miss Thelma turned her chin to the sound. She smiled. "That's what keeps *me* from being forgot."

She closed her eyes, allowing my mother to work on them. She drew a breath and eased lower into the bed.

"But I didn't hold my family together," I blurted out.

My mother raised a finger to her lips for silence.

To my Charley on his wedding day—

I know you think these notes are silly. I have watched you scrunch your face over the years when I give them to you. But understand that sometimes I want to tell you something and I want to get it just right. Putting it down on paper helps me do that. I wish I had been a better writer. I wish I had gone to college. If I had, I think I would have studied English and maybe my vocabulary would have improved. So many times I feel I am using the same words over and over, like a woman wearing the same dress every day. So boring!

What I want to say to you, Charley, is you are marrying a wonderful girl. I think of Catherine in many ways like I think of Roberta. Like a daughter. She is sweet and patient. You should be the same with her, Charley.

Here is what you are going to find out

about marriage: you have to work at it together. And you have to <u>love</u> three things. You have to love

1) Each other.
2) Your children (When you have some! Hint! Hint!).
3) Your marriage.

What I mean by that last one is, there may be times that you fight, and sometimes you and Catherine won't even like each other. But those are the times you have to love your marriage. It's like a third party. Look at your wedding photos. Look at any memories you've made. And if you believe in those memories, they will pull you back together.

I'm very proud of you today, Charley. I am putting this in your tuxedo pocket because I know how you lose things.

I love you every day!

Mom

(from Chick Benetto's papers, circa 1974)

Reaching the Top

I HAVEN'T TOLD YOU YET about the best and worst thing that ever happened to me professionally. I made it to the end of the baseball rainbow: the World Series. I was only twenty-three. The Pirates' backup catcher broke his ankle in early September and they needed a replacement, so I was called up. I still remember the day I walked into that carpeted locker room. I couldn't believe the size of it. I called Catherine from a pay phone—we'd been married for six months—and I kept repeating, "It's *unbelievable*."

A few weeks later, the Pirates won the pennant. It would be a lie to say I was in any way responsible; they were in first place when I arrived. I did catch four innings in one playoff game, and in my second at-bat I smacked a ball to deep right field. It was caught, and I was out, but I remember thinking, "That's a start. I can hit this stuff."

It wasn't a start. Not for me. We reached the World Series, but were beaten in five games by the Baltimore Orioles. I never even got to bat. The last game was a 5–0 defeat, and after the final out, I stood on the dugout steps and watched the Baltimore players run onto the field and celebrate, throwing themselves into a giant pile by the pitcher's mound. To others they looked ecstatic, but to me they looked relieved, like the pressure was finally off.

I never saw that look again, but I still dream about it sometimes. I see myself in that pile.

HAD THE PIRATES won the championship, there would have been a parade in Pittsburgh. Instead, because we lost on the road, we went to a Baltimore bar and closed it down. Defeat had to be washed away by booze in those days, and we washed ours away thoroughly. As the newest guy on the team, I mostly listened to the older players grumble. I drank what I was supposed to drink. I cursed when they all cursed. It was dawn when we staggered out of the place.

We flew home a few hours later—in those days, everybody flew commercial—and most of us took hangover naps. They had taxis lined up for us at the airport. We shook hands. We said, "See ya next year." The doors shut in one cab after another, *thump, thump, thump.*

The following March, in spring training, I blew out my knee. I was sliding into third base, and my foot jammed and the fielder tripped over me and I felt a snap like I'd never felt before. The doctor said I tore the anterior, posterior, and medial collateral ligaments—the trifecta of knee injuries.

In time, I healed. I resumed playing baseball. But for the next six years, I never came close to the major leagues again, no matter how hard I tried, no matter how well I thought I was doing. It was as if the magic had washed off of me. The only evidence I had of my time in the big leagues was the newspaper box scores from 1973 and my baseball card, with a photo of me holding a bat, looking serious, my name in block letters, the smell of bubble gum permanently attached. The company shipped me two boxes of those cards. I sent one box to my father. I kept the other.

They call a short stay in baseball "a cup of coffee," and that's what I had, but it was a cup of coffee at the best table in the best joint in town.

Which, of course, was good and bad.

ℚℐ YOU SEE, I was more alive in those six weeks with the Pirates than I ever felt before or since. The spotlight had made me feel immortal. I missed the huge, carpeted locker room. I missed walking through airports with my teammates, feeling the eyes of the fans as we passed. I missed the crowds in those big stadiums, the flashbulbs, the roaring cheers—the majesty of the whole thing. I missed it bitterly. So did my father. We shared a thirst to return; unspoken, undeniable.

And so I clung to baseball long after I should have quit. I went from minor-league city to minor-league city, still believing, as athletes often do, that I would be the first to defy the aging process. I dragged Catherine with me all over the country. We had apartments in Portland, Jacksonville, Albuquerque, Fayetteville, and Omaha. During her pregnancy, she had three different doctors.

In the end, Maria was born in Pawtucket, Rhode Island,

two hours after a game attended by maybe eighty people before rain sent them scattering. I had to wait for a cab to get to the hospital. I was almost as wet as my daughter when she came into the world.

I quit baseball not long after that.

And nothing I tried ever came close. I attempted my own business, which only lost me money. I looked around for coaching positions, but couldn't find any. In the end, a guy offered me a job in sales. His company made plastic bottles for food and pharmaceuticals, and I took it. The work was dull. The hours were tedious. Even worse, I only got the job because they figured I could tell baseball stories and maybe close a deal in the frothy hubris of men talking sports.

It's funny. I met a man once who did a lot of mountain climbing. I asked him which was harder, ascending or descending? He said without a doubt descending, because ascending you were so focused on reaching the top, you avoided mistakes.

"The backside of a mountain is a fight against human nature," he said. "You have to care as much about yourself on the way down as you did on the way up."

I could spend a lot of time talking about my life after baseball. But that pretty much says it.

෧෮ NOT SURPRISINGLY, MY father faded with my athletic career. Oh, he came to see the baby a few times. But he was not as fascinated by a grandchild as I hoped he would be. As time passed, we had less and less to talk about. He sold his liquor stores and bought a half interest in a distributorship, which more than paid his bills without requiring much attendance. It's funny. Even though I needed a job, he never once offered one. I guess he'd spent too much time molding me to be different to allow me to be the same.

It wouldn't have mattered. Baseball was our common country, and without it, we drifted like two boats with the oars pulled in. He bought a condo in a suburb of Pittsburgh, joined a golf club, developed a mild form of diabetes, and had to watch his diet and give himself shots.

And just as effortlessly as he had surfaced beneath those gray college skies, so did my old man slide back into foggy absentia, the occasional phone call, the Christmas card.

You might ask if he ever explained what happened between him and my mother. He didn't. He simply said, "It didn't work out between us." If I pressed him, he would add, "You wouldn't understand." The worst he ever said about my mother was, "She's a hardheaded woman."

It was as if they had made this pact to never speak about what drove them apart. But I asked them both the question, and only my father lowered his eyes when he answered.

The Second Visit Ends

"*P*OSEY," MISS THELMA WHISPERED, "I'm gonna visit with my grandchildren for a spell."

She looked much better than when she'd rung the bell at my mother's house. Her face was smooth and her eyes and lips were done nicely. My mother had brushed out her dyed orange tresses, and for the first time I realized that Miss Thelma was an attractive woman, and must have been a knockout when she was young.

My mother laid a kiss on Miss Thelma's cheek, then closed her bag and motioned for me to follow. We stepped into the hallway, where a little girl with her hair in braids was heading toward us, clomping her feet.

"Grandma?" she said. "Are you 'wake?"

I stepped back, but she walked right past us, never looking up. She was followed by a little boy—maybe her brother?—who stopped in the doorway and put a finger in his mouth. I reached out and waved a hand before his face. Nothing. It was clear we were invisible to them.

"Mom," I stammered. "What's going on?"

She was looking at Miss Thelma, whose granddaughter was now on the bed. They were playing some kind of pat-a-cake. My mother had tears in her eyes.

"Is Miss Thelma dying, too?"

"Soon," my mother said.

I stepped in front of her.

"Mom. Please?"

"She called for me, Charley."

We both looked toward the bed.

"Miss Thelma? She summoned you?"

"No, sweetheart. I came to her mind, that's all. I was a thought. She wished I was still around and could help her look pretty, not as sick, so here I was."

"A *thought*?" I looked down. "I'm lost."

My mother moved closer. Her voice softened. "Have you ever dreamt of someone who's gone, Charley, but in the dream you have a new conversation? The world you enter then is not so far from the world I'm in now."

She put one hand on mine. "When someone is in your heart, they're never truly gone. They can come back to you, even at unlikely times."

On the bed, the little girl played with Miss Thelma's hair. Miss Thelma grinned and glanced over at us.

"Do you remember the old lady Golinski?" my mother said.

I remembered. A patient at the hospital. Terminal illness. She was dying. But she used to tell my mother every day about people who "visited" her. People from her past with whom she spoke and laughed. My mother recounted this at the dinner table, how she'd peek in the room and see the old lady Golinski with her eyes closed, smiling and mumbling in some invisible conversation. My father called her "crazy." She died a week later.

"She wasn't crazy," my mother said now.

"Then Miss Thelma is . . ."

"Close." My mother's eyes narrowed. "It's easier to talk to the dead the closer you get."

I felt a cold flush from my shoulders to my feet.

"Does that mean I'm . . ."

I meant to say "dying." I meant to say "gone."

"You're my son," she whispered. "That's what you are."

I swallowed. "How much time do I have?"

"Some," she said.

"Not a lot?"

"What's a lot?"

"I don't know, Mom. Will I be with you forever, or will you be gone in a minute?"

"You can find something truly important in a minute," she said.

Suddenly, all the glass in Miss Thelma's house exploded, windows, mirrors, TV screens. The shattering pieces flew around us as if we stood in the vortex of a hurricane. A voice from outside thundered over it all.

"CHARLES BENETTO! I KNOW YOU CAN HEAR ME! ANSWER ME!"

"What do I do?" I screamed to my mother.

She blinked calmly as the glass swirled around her.

"That's up to you, Charley," she said.

IV. Night

The Sunlight Fades

"*O*NCE HEAVEN IS DONE WITH GRANDMA, WE'D LIKE HER BACK, THANKS." My daughter had written that in the guest book at my mother's funeral, the kind of assumptive yet incongruent thing a teenager comes up with. But seeing my mother again, hearing her explain how this "dead" world worked, how she was called back to people by their memories of her—well, maybe Maria was onto something.

The glass storm of Miss Thelma's house had passed; I'd had to squeeze my eyes shut to make it stop. Shards of glass poked in my skin and I tried to brush them free, but even that seemed to require great effort. I was weakening, withering. This day with my mother was losing its light.

"Am I going to die?" I asked.

"I don't know, Charley. Only God knows that."

"Is this heaven?"

"This is Pepperville Beach. Don't you remember?"

"If I'm dead . . . If I die . . . do I get to be with you?"

She grinned. "Oh, so *now* you want to be with me."

Maybe that sounds cold to you. But my mother was just being my mother, a little funny, a little teasing, the way she'd be had we spent this day together *before* she'd died.

She was also justified. So many times, I had chosen *not* to be with her. Too busy. Too tired. Don't feel like dealing with it. *Church?* No thanks. *Dinner?* Sorry. *Come down to visit?* Can't do it, maybe next week.

You count the hours you could have spent with your mother. It's a lifetime in itself.

☙ SHE TOOK MY hand now. After Miss Thelma's, we simply walked forward and the scenery changed and we eased through a series of brief appearances in people's lives. Some I recognized as my mother's old friends. Some were men I barely knew, men who had once admired her: a butcher named Armando, a tax attorney named Howard, a flat-nosed watch repairman named Gerhard. My mother spent only a moment with each, smiling or sitting in front of them.

"So they're thinking about you now?" I said.

"Mmm," she said, nodding.

"You go everywhere you're thought of?"

"No," she said. "Not everywhere."

We appeared near a man gazing out a window. Then another man in a hospital bed.

"So many," I said.

"They were just men, Charley. Decent men. Some were widowers."

"Did you go out with them?"

"No."

"Did they ask?"

"Many times."

"Why are you seeing them now?"

"Oh, a woman's prerogative, I guess." She placed her hands together and touched her nose, hiding a small smile. "It's still nice to be thought about, you know."

I studied her face. There was no doubting her beauty, even in her late seventies, when she had taken on a more wrinkled elegance, her eyes behind glasses, her hair—once the blue-black of midnight—now the silver of a cloudy afternoon sky. These men had seen her as a woman. But I had never seen her that way. I had never known her as Pauline, the name her parents had given her, or as Posey, the name her friends had given her; only as Mom, the name I had given her. I could only see her carrying dinner to the table with kitchen mitts, or carpooling us to the bowling alley.

"Why didn't you marry again?" I asked.

"Charley." She narrowed her eyes. "Come on."

"No. I'm serious. After we grew up—weren't you lonely?"

She looked away. "Sometimes. But then you and Roberta had kids, and that gave me grandkids, and I had the ladies here and—oh, you know, Charley. The years pass."

I watched her turn her palms up and smile. I had forgotten the small joy of listening to my mother talk about herself.

"Life goes quickly, doesn't it, Charley?"

"Yeah," I mumbled.

"It's such a shame to waste time. We always think we have so much of it."

I thought about the days I had handed over to a bottle. The nights I couldn't remember. The mornings I slept through. All that time spent running from myself.

"Do you remember—" She started laughing. "When I dressed you as a mummy for Halloween? And it rained?"

I looked down. *"You ruined my life."*

Even then, I thought, blaming someone else.

  "YOU SHOULD EAT some supper," she said.

And with that, we were back in her kitchen, at the round table, one last time. There was fried chicken and yellow rice and roasted eggplant, all hot, all familiar, dishes she'd cooked for my sister and me a hundred times. But unlike the stunned sensation I'd felt earlier in this room, now I was agitated, unnerved, as if I knew something bad was coming. She glanced at me, concerned, and I tried to deflect her attention.

"Tell me about your family," I said.

"Charley," she said. "I've told you that stuff."

My head was pounding.

"Tell me again."

And so she did. She told me about her parents, both immigrants, who died before I was born. She told me about her two uncles and her crazy aunt who refused to learn English and still believed in family curses. She told me about her cousins, Joe and Eddie, who lived on the other coast. There was usually one small anecdote that identified each person. ("She was deathly afraid of dogs." "He tried to join the Navy when he was fifteen.") And it seemed critical now that I match the name with the detail. Roberta and I used to roll our eyes when she launched into these stories. But years later, after the funeral, Maria had asked me questions about the family— who was related to whom—and I struggled. I couldn't remember. A big chunk of our history had been buried with my mother. You should never let your past disappear that way.

So this time, I listened intently as my mother went through each branch of the tree, bending back a finger for every person she recounted. Finally, when she finished, she pushed her hands together, and the fingers—like the characters—intertwined.

"Annnyhow," she half sang. "That was—"

"I missed you, Mom."

The words just spilled out of me. She smiled, but she didn't answer. She seemed to consider the sentence, gathering my intent, as if pulling in a fisherman's net.

Then, with the sun setting into whatever horizon of whatever world we were in, she ticked her tongue and said, "We have one more stop to make, Charley."

The Day He Wanted Back

I NEED TO TELL YOU NOW about the last time I saw my mother alive, and the thing that I did.

It was eight years earlier, at her seventy-ninth birthday party. She had joked that people had better come, because starting next year "I'm not going to tell anyone it's my birthday ever again." Of course she said this at sixty-nine and fifty-nine and maybe even twenty-nine.

The party was a lunch at her house on a Saturday afternoon. In attendance were my wife and daughter; my sister, Roberta, and her husband, Elliot; their three kids (the youngest of which, five-year-old Roxanne, now wore ballerina slippers wherever *she* went); plus a good two dozen people from the old neighborhood, including the elderly women whose hair my mother washed and set. Many of these women were in poor health; one came in a wheelchair. Still, they had all been recently coiffed, their hair sprayed like helmets, and I wondered if my mother hadn't organized the party just so the ladies had a reason to primp.

"I want Grandma to do my makeup, OK?" Maria said, bounding up to me, her fourteen-year-old body still coltish and awkward.

"Why?" I said.

" 'Cause I want her to. She said if it was OK with you, she would."

I looked at Catherine. She shrugged. Maria rabbit-punched me in the arm.

"Please-please-please-please-please?"

I have spoken enough about how bleak my life felt after baseball. I should mention that Maria was the exception to all that. I found my greatest joy in her. I tried to be a decent father. I tried to pay attention to the little things. I wiped the ketchup off her face after French fries. I sat beside her at her small desk, pencil in hand, helping her do math problems. I sent her back upstairs when, as an eleven-year-old, she came down wearing a halter top. And I was always quick to throw her a ball or take her to the local YMCA for swimming lessons, happy to keep her a tomboy as long as possible.

I would later learn, after I fell out of her life, that she wrote about sports for her college newspaper. And in that mixing of words and athletics, I realized how your mother and father pass through you to your children, like it or not.

AS THE PARTY continued, plates clanked and music played. The room hummed with chatter. My mother read her cards out loud as if they were congratulatory telegrams from foreign dignitaries, even the cheap, pastel-colored ones with rabbits on the front ("Just thought I'd hop in to say . . .

Hope your birthday is a real *thumper*!"). When she finished she would turn the card open so everyone could see, and she'd blow a kiss to the sender: *"Mmmwah!"*

Sometime after the cards, but before the cake and gifts, the phone rang. The phone could ring a long time in my mother's house because she wouldn't rush what she was doing to answer; she would finish vacuuming the last corner or spraying the last window, as if it didn't count until you picked it up.

Since nobody was getting it, I did.

If I had my life to do over again, I would have let it ring.

ଚ୭ "HELLO?" I YELLED over the din.

My mother still used a Princess phone. The cord was twenty feet long because she liked to walk around as she talked.

"Hello?" I said again. I pressed the receiver closer to my ear.

"Hel-looo?"

I was about to hang up when I heard a man clear his throat. Then my father said, "Chick? That you?"

ଚ୭ AT FIRST I didn't answer. I was stunned. Although my mother's phone number had never changed, it was hard to believe my father was calling it. His departure from this house had been so sudden and destructive, hearing his voice seemed like a man walking back into a burning building.

"Yeah, it's me," I whispered.

"I've been trying to find you. I called your house and your office. I took a chance you might be—"

"It's Mom's birthday."

"Oh, right," he said.

"Did you want to speak to her?"

I had rushed into that sentence. I could feel my father rolling his eyes.

"Chick, I was talking with Pete Garner."

"Pete Garner—"

"From the Pirates."

"Yeah?"

I walked the phone away from the guests. As I cupped the receiver with my free hand, I glanced at two old women sitting on the couch, eating tuna salad from paper plates.

"They got their Old Timers game, right?" my father said. "And Pete tells me Freddie Gonzalez bailed out. Some crap with his paperwork."

"I don't get why—"

"It's too late for them to make calls for a replacement. So I say to Pete, 'Hey, Chick's around.'"

"Dad. I'm not around."

"You can be. He don't know where you're at."

"An Old Timers game?"

"So he says, 'Oh, yeah? Chick is?' And I say, "Yeah. In good shape, too—'"

"Dad—"

"And so Pete says—"

"Dad—"

I knew where this was going. I knew it immediately. The only person who had a harder time giving up my baseball career than me was my father.

"Pete says they'll put you on the roster. All's you got to do is—"

"Dad, I only played—"

"Get up here—"

"Six weeks in the majors—"

"Around ten A.M.—"

"I only played—"

"And then—"

"You can't do an Old Timers game with—"

"What's your problem, Chick?"

I hate that question. *What's your problem?* There is no good answer except, "I don't have a problem." Which clearly was not true.

I sighed. "They said they'd put me on the roster?"

"That's what I'm saying—"

"To play?"

"Are you deaf? That's what I'm saying."

"And this is when?"

"Tomorrow. The guys from the organization will be there and—"

"Tomorrow, Dad?"

"Tomorrow. What?"

"It's like, three o'clock already—"

"You're in the dugout. You bump into these guys. You strike up a conversation."

"I bump into who?"

"Whoever. Anderson. Molina. Mike Junez, the trainer, the bald guy? You make it a goddamn point to bump into them. You get to talking, you never know."

"What?"

"Something opens up. A coaching spot. A batting instructor. Something in the minors. You get a foot in the door—"

"Why would they want me—"

"That's how these things—"

"I haven't swung a bat in—"

"—Happen, that's how they happen, Chick. You get a foot in the door—"

"But I—"

"It's who you know when these jobs open—"

"Dad. I *have* a job."

A pause. My father could hurt you more with a pause than any man I'd ever known.

"Look," he said, exhaling. "I finagled an opening. You want this or not?"

His voice had shifted, the fighter angering, balling his fists. He had dismissed my current existence as swiftly as I wished I could. It made me recoil, and in recoiling, of course, a fight is lost.

"Just get your butt out here, OK?" he said.

"It's Mom's birthday."

"Not tomorrow, it ain't."

৩৩ LOOKING BACK ON that conversation, there are many things I wished I'd asked. Did he give a hoot that his ex-wife was having a birthday? Did he want to know how she was feeling? Who was there? What the house looked like? If she ever thought about him? Fondly? Badly? At all?

There are a lot of things I wished I'd asked him. Instead, I said I'd call him back. I hung up the phone. And I let the opportunity my father had "finagled" dance around my head.

I thought about it as my mother sliced her vanilla layer cake and put each piece on a paper plate. I thought about it as she opened her presents. I thought about it as Catherine, Maria, and I posed around her for a photo—Maria now covered in purple eye shadow—and my mom's friend Edith held up the camera and said, "*One, two* . . . uch, wait, this thing, I can never figure it out."

And even as we stood there forcing our smiles, I was picturing my swing.

I tried to focus. I tried to wrap my mother's birthday party around me. But my father, a thief in many ways, had robbed me of my concentration. Before the paper plates were tossed, I was down in the basement, on the phone, booking the last plane out.

My mother used to start her sentences with "Be a good boy . . . ," as in "Be a good boy and take out the garbage . . ." or "Be a good boy and run to the store . . ." But with one phone call, the good boy I had been when I arrived that day had taken a powder, and another boy had taken his place.

ﾝ I HAD TO lie to everyone there. It wasn't hard. I wore a pager for work, and I called it from the downstairs phone, then went upstairs quickly. When the pager went off in front of Catherine, I acted annoyed, grumbling about them "bothering me on a Saturday."

I faked the return phone call. Faked my dismay. Faked a story about having to fly to a client who could only do the meeting on a Sunday, and wasn't it awful?

"They can't wait?" my mother asked.

"I know, it's ridiculous," I said.

"But we're having brunch tomorrow."

"Look, what do you want me to do?"

"You can't call them back?"

"No, Mom," I snapped. "I can't call them back."

She looked down. I exhaled. The more you defend a lie, the angrier you become.

An hour later, a cab pulled up. I grabbed my bag. I hugged Catherine and Maria, who forced smiles that were really half-frowns. I yelled a good-bye into the gathering. The group yelled back, "So long . . . Bye . . . Good luck . . ."

I heard my mother's voice last, above the others: "Love you, Char—"

The door shut mid-sentence.

And I never saw her again.

Times My Mother Stood Up for Me

"But what do you know about running a restaurant?" my wife says.

"It's a sports bar," I say.

We are sitting at our dining room table. My mother is there as well, playing peekaboo with little Maria. This is after I've quit baseball. A friend wants me to partner in a new business.

"But isn't it hard to run a bar?" Catherine says. "Aren't there things you have to know about?"

"He knows that stuff," I say.

"What do you think, Mom?" Catherine asks.

My mother takes Maria's hands and flops them up and down.

"Would you have to work nights, Charley?" she asks.

"What?"

"Nights. Would you have to work nights?"

"I'm the investor, Mom. I'm not gonna wait tables."

"It's a lot of money," Catherine says.

"If you don't invest money, you can't make money," I say.

"Isn't there something besides this?" Catherine says.

I exhale loudly. In truth, I don't know what there is. When you play sports, you train yourself not to think too much about anything else. I can't imagine myself behind a desk. This is a bar. I know about bars. I have already begun a reliance on alcohol as part of my daily existence and secretly there is

*appeal in having it so handy. Plus, the place has the word
"sports" in it.*

"Where is it?" my mother asks.

"About a half an hour from here."

"How often would you have to go?"

"I don't know."

"But not at night?"

"Why do you keep asking about nights?"

*She wiggles her fingers in Maria's face. "You have a
daughter, Charley."*

I shake my head. "I know, Mom, OK?"

*Catherine rises. She clears the dishes. "It scares me, that's
all. I'm just being honest."*

*I slump. I stare down. When I look up, my mother is
watching me. She puts a finger under her chin and lifts it
slightly, telling me, in her way, that I should do the same.*

*"You know what I think?" she announces. "I think you have
to try things in life. Is this something you believe in, Charley?"*

I nod yes.

*"Belief, hard work, love—you have those things, you can do
anything."*

*I sit up. My wife shrugs. The mood has changed. The odds
have improved.*

A few months later, the sports bar opens.

Two years later, it goes out of business.

*Apparently, you need more than those three things. At least
in my world, if not hers.*

The Game

I STAYED IN A BEST WESTERN hotel the night before the Old Timers game, which reminded me of my playing days and the road trips we took. I couldn't sleep. I wondered how many people would be in the ballpark. I wondered if I could even make contact with a pitch. At 5:30 A.M., I got out of bed to try some stretching. The red light on my phone was blinking. I called the front desk. It rang at least twenty times.

"I have a message light on," I said when someone finally answered.

"One sec . . . ," the voice groaned. "Yeah. There's a package for you."

I went downstairs. The clerk handed me an old shoe box. It had my name taped on top. He yawned. I opened it.

My cleats.

Apparently, my father had kept them all these years. He must have dropped them off sometime during the night, without even phoning the room. I looked for a note, but there was nothing else in the box. Just my shoes, with all their old scrapes.

I ARRIVED AT the ballpark early. I had the cab drop me off, out of habit, near the players' entrance, but the guard directed me to the employee gate, where the beer and hot dog vendors enter. The stadium was empty and the halls smelled of sausage grease. It was strange, returning to this place. I had wanted, for so many years, to earn my way back as a player. Now I was part of a promotion, Old Timers Day, a few innings of free nostalgia, a way to sell tickets—like Cap Day, Ball Day, or Fireworks Day.

I found my way to an auxiliary locker room where we were supposed to dress. An attendant at the door checked my name off a list and gave me my uniform for the day.

"Where can I . . . ?"

"Anyplace over there," he motioned, pointing to a row of metal lockers, greasepaint blue.

Two white-haired guys were talking in the corner. They gave me a chin nod without stopping their conversation. It felt awkward, like going to a high school reunion for someone else's class. Then again, I'd had six weeks in the major leagues. It wasn't like I'd made lifelong friends.

ɷ MY UNIFORM HAD "BENETTO" stitched across the back, although upon careful inspection, I could see the fabric shading from an old name that had been there before. I pulled the top over my head. I wiggled my arms through the sleeves.

When I tugged it down, I turned, and Willie "Bomber" Jackson was standing a few feet away.

Everyone knew Jackson. He was a terrific hitter, famous for both his power and his cockiness at the plate. Once, during the playoffs, he pointed his bat to the right-field fence, calling his shot, and then delivered with a towering home run. You only have to do this once in your career to be immortalized, what with the replays they have on TV. And he was.

Now he sat on a stool next to me. I had never played with Jackson. He was pudgy, almost inflated-looking in his blue velour sweatsuit, but there was still something regal about him. He nodded at me and I nodded back.

"What's up?" he said.

"Chick Benetto," I said, offering my hand. He grabbed the inner fingers and yanked them. He never said his name. It was understood he didn't have to.

"So, Chuck, what're you doing these days?"

I didn't correct his pronunciation. I said I was in "marketing."

"And you?" I asked. "Still broadcasting?"

"Mmm. Little bit. Mostly investments now."

I nodded. "Cool. Yeah. Good move. Investments."

"Mutual funds," he said. "Some shelters, unit trusts, stuff like that. Mostly mutuals."

I nodded again. I felt stupid for already wearing my uniform.

"You into the market?" he said.

I flipped my palm. "You know, here and there." That was a lie. I was neither here nor there in the market.

He studied me, moving his jaw.

"Well, lookit. I can hook you up."

For a moment there was something to this, the famous Jackson willing to hook me up, and I began in my mind to come up with money I did not have. But as he reached in his pocket, presumably for a business card, someone yelled "JACKSON, YOU FAT FART!" We both spun and there was Spike Alexander, and he and Jackson embraced so hard they almost tumbled into me. I had to step out of the way.

A minute later they were across the room, surrounded by others, and that was it for my time in mutual funds.

THE OLD TIMERS game was played an hour before the real game, which meant the stands were mostly empty when we began. An organ sounded. The PA announcer welcomed the sparse crowd. We were introduced alphabetically, beginning with an outfielder named Rusty Allenback who played in the late 1940s, followed by Benny "Bobo" Barbosa, a popular infielder from the 1960s with one of those huge, wide grins. He ran out waving. The fans were still clapping for him when my name was called. The announcer said, "From the pennant-winning team of 1973 . . . ," and you could hear a tingle of anticipation and then "Catcher Charles 'Chick' Benetto," and there was a sudden drop in volume, enthusiasm melting to politeness.

I darted out of the dugout and almost ran up Barbosa's legs. I was trying to take my place before the applause died, to avoid that embarrassing silence where you can hear your own feet on the gravelly sand. Somewhere in that crowd was my old man, although when I pictured him, his arms were crossed. No clapping from the home team.

❧ AND THEN THE game itself. It was like a train station in the dugout, guys shuffling in and out, grabbing bats, bumping around each other as their cleats rang on the concrete floor. I had one inning catching, which was plenty, because squatting down after all those years had my thighs burning as early as the third pitch. I kept shifting my weight from foot to foot, until one batter, a tall, hairy-armed guy named Teddy Slaughter, said, "Hey, pal, you wanna stop hopping around back there?"

To the arriving crowd, I suppose it looked like baseball. Eight fielders, one pitcher, one batter, one umpire dressed in black. But we were far from the fluid, powerful dance of our younger days. We were slow now. Clunky. Our swings were leaden, and our throws were high and loping, too much air beneath them.

In our dugout, there were big-bellied men who had clearly surrendered to the aging process, and who cracked jokes like, "Jesus, somebody get me some *oxygen!*" And then there were guys who still held to the code of taking all games seriously. I sat next to an old Puerto Rican outfielder, he had to be at least sixty, who kept spitting tobacco juice on the floor and mumbling, "Here we go, babies, here we go . . ."

When I finally came to bat, the stadium was less than half full. I took a few practice swings and then stepped into the batter's box. The sun went behind a cloud. I heard a vendor yell. I felt perspiration on my neck. I shifted on my feet. And even though I had done this a million times in my life—gripped the bat handle, raised my shoulders, set my jaw, narrowed my gaze—my heart was racing. I think I just wanted to survive for more than a few seconds. The first pitch came in. I let it go. The umpire called, "Ball one!" and I wanted to thank him.

∞ DO YOU EVER think while something is happening, about what's happening someplace else? My mother, after the divorce, would stand on the back porch at sunset, smoking a cigarette, and she'd say, "Charley, right now, as the sun is going down here, it's coming up someplace else in the world. Australia or China or someplace. You can look it up in the encyclopedia."

She'd blow smoke and stare down the row of square backyards, with their laundry poles and swing sets.

"It's such a big world," she'd say, wistfully. "Something is always happening somewhere."

She was right about that. Something is always happening somewhere. So when I stood at the plate in that Old Timers game, staring at a pitcher whose hair was gray, and when he threw what used to be his fastball but what now was just a pitch that floated in toward my chest, and when I swung and made contact and heard the familiar *thwock* and I dropped my bat and began to run, convinced that I had done something fabulous, forgetting my old gauges, forgetting that my arms and legs lacked the power they once had, forgetting that as you age, the walls get farther away, and when I looked up and saw what I had first thought to be a solid hit, maybe a home run, now coming down just beyond the infield toward the waiting glove of the second baseman, no more than a pop-up, a wet firecracker, a dud, and a voice in my head yelled, "Drop it! Drop it!" as that second baseman squeezed his glove around my final offering to this maddening game— just as all that was happening, my mother, as she once noted, had something else happening back in Pepperville Beach.

Her clock radio was playing big band music. Her pillows had been freshly plumped. And her body was crumpled like a broken doll on the floor of her bedroom, where she had come looking for her new red glasses and collapsed.

A massive heart attack.

She was taking her last breaths.

*W*HEN THE OLD TIMERS game was finished, we walked back down the tunnel, passing the current players. We took each other's measure. They were young and smooth-skinned. We were fat and balding. I nodded at a muscular guy carrying a catcher's mask. It was like watching myself going out as I was coming in.

Inside the locker room, I packed up quickly. Some of us took showers, but it seemed silly. We hadn't really worked that hard. I folded my uniform top and kept it as a souvenir. I zipped my bag shut. I sat for a few minutes, fully dressed. Then there didn't seem to be much point.

I exited the way I'd come in, through the employees' entrance. And there was my father, smoking a cigarette and looking up at the sky. He seemed surprised to see me.

"Thanks for the cleats," I said, holding them up.

"What are you doing out here?" he said, annoyed. "Can't you find someone to talk to in there?"

I spurted out a sarcastic breath. "I dunno, Dad. I guess I came out to say hello. I haven't seen you in like two years."

"Jesus." He shook his head in disgust. "How are you gonna get back in the game talking to *me*?"

Chick Finds Out His Mom Is Gone

"*H*ELLO?"

My wife's voice sounded shaky, disturbed.

"Hey, it's me," I said. "Sorry I—"

"Oh, Chick, oh, God, we didn't know where to *reach* you."

I had been ready with my lies—the client, the meeting, all of it—but they fell now like bricks.

"What's the matter?" I said.

"Your mom. Oh, my God, Chick. Where were you? We didn't . . ."

"What? What?"

She started crying, gasping.

"Tell me," I said. *"What?"*

"It was a heart attack. Maria found her."

"Wha . . . ?"

"Your mom . . . She died."

I HOPE YOU never hear those words. *Your mom. She died.* They are different than other words. They are too big to fit in your ears. They belong to some strange, heavy, powerful language that pounds away at the side of your head, a wrecking ball coming at you again and again, until finally, the words crack a hole large enough to fit inside your brain. And in so doing, they split you apart.

"Where?"

"At the house."

"Where, I mean, when?"

Suddenly, details seemed extremely important. Details were something to grab on to, a way to insert myself into the story. "How did she—"

"Chick," Catherine said softly, "just come home, OK?"

I rented a car. I drove through the night. I drove with my shock and grief in the backseat, and my guilt in the front. I reached Pepperville Beach just before sunrise. I pulled into the driveway. I shut the engine. The sky was a rotted purple. My car smelled of beer. As I sat there, watching the dawn rise around me, I realized I hadn't called my father to tell him of my mother's death. I sensed, deep down, that I would never see him again.

And I never did.

I lost both parents on the same day, one to shame, one to shadow.

A Third and Final Visit

*M*Y MOTHER AND I WALKED now through a town I had never seen. It was unremarkable, a gas station on one corner, a small convenience store on the other. The telephone poles and the bark of the trees were the same cardboard color, and most of the trees had dropped their leaves.

We stopped in front of a two-story apartment building. It was pale yellow brick.

"Where are we?" I said.

My mother checked the horizon. The sun had already set.

"You should have had more dinner," she said.

I rolled my eyes. "Come on."

"What? I like knowing you've eaten, that's all. You have to take care of yourself, Charley."

I saw in her expression that old, unshakable mountain of concern. And I realized when you look at your mother, you are looking at the purest love you will ever know.

"I wish we'd done this before, Mom, you know?"

"You mean before I died?"

My voice went timid. "Yeah."

"I was here."

"I know."

"You were busy."

I shuddered at that word. It seemed so hollow now. I saw a wave of resignation pass over her face. I believe, at that moment, we were both thinking how things might be different if we did them over.

"Charley," she asked, "was I a good mother?"

I opened my mouth to answer, but a blinding flash erased her from sight. I felt heat on my face, as if the sun were baking down on it. Then, once again, that booming voice:

"CHARLES BENETTO. OPEN YOUR EYES!"

I blinked hard. Suddenly, I was blocks behind my mother, as if she'd kept walking and I'd stopped. I blinked again. She was even farther ahead. I could barely see her anymore. I stretched forward, my fingers straining, my shoulders pulling from their sockets. Everything was spinning. I felt myself trying to call her name, the word vibrating in my throat. It took all the strength I had.

And then she was with me again, taking my hand, all calm, as if nothing had happened. We glided back to where we'd been.

"One more stop," she repeated.

SHE TURNED ME toward the pale yellow building and instantly we were inside it, a low-ceilinged apartment, heavily furnished. The bedroom was small. The wallpaper was avocado green. A painting of vineyards hung on the wall and a cross was over the bed. In the corner there was a champagne wooden dressing table beneath a large mirror. And before that mirror sat a dark-haired woman, wearing a bathrobe the color of pink grapefruit.

She appeared to be in her seventies, with a long, narrow nose and prominent cheekbones beneath her sagging olive skin. She ran a brush through her hair slowly, absently, looking down at the counter.

My mother stepped up behind her. There was no greeting. Instead she put her hands out and they melted into the hands of the woman, one holding the brush, the other following the strokes with a flattening palm.

The woman glanced up, as if checking her reflection in the mirror, but her eyes were smoky and far away. I think she was seeing my mother.

Neither said a word.

"Mom," I finally whispered. "Who is she?"

My mother turned, her hands in the woman's hair.

"She's your father's wife."

Times I Did *Not* Stand Up for My Mother

Take the shovel, the minister said. He said it with his eyes. I was to toss dirt onto my mother's coffin, which was half-lowered into the grave. My mother, the minister explained, had witnessed this custom at Jewish funerals and had requested it for her own. She felt it helped mourners accept that the body was gone and they should remember the spirit. I could hear my father chiding her, saying, "Posey, I swear, you make it up as you go along."

I took the shovel like a child being handed a rifle. I looked to my sister, Roberta, who wore a black veil over her face and was visibly trembling. I looked to my wife, who was staring at her feet, tears streaming down her cheeks, her right hand rhythmically smoothing our daughter's hair. Only Maria looked at me. And her eyes seemed to say, "Don't do it, Dad. Give it back."

In baseball, a player can tell when he's holding his own bat and when he's holding someone else's. Which is how I felt with that shovel in my hands. It was someone else's. It did not belong to me. It belonged to a son who didn't lie to his mother. It belonged to a son whose last words to her were not in anger. It belonged to a son who hadn't raced off to satisfy the latest whim of his distant old man, who, in keeping the record intact, was absent from this family gathering, having decided, "It's better if I'm not there, I don't want to upset anybody."

That son would have stayed that weekend, sleeping with his wife in the guest room, having Sunday brunch with the family. That son would have been there when his mother collapsed. That son might have saved her.

But that son was not around.

This son swallowed, and did what he was told: He shoveled dirt onto the coffin. It landed with a messy spread, a few gravelly pieces making noise against the polished wood. And even though it was her idea, I heard my mother's voice saying, "Oh, Charley. How could you?"

Everything Explained

She's your father's wife.

How can I explain that sentence? I can't. I can only tell you what my mother's spirit told me, standing in that strange apartment with a painting of vineyards on the wall.

"She's your father's wife. They met during the war. Your father was stationed in Italy. He told you that, right?"

Many times. Italy, late 1944. The Apennine mountains and the Po Valley, not far from Bologna.

"She lived in a village there. She was poor. He was a soldier. You know how those things go. Your father, in those days, was very, I don't know, what's the word? Bold?"

My mother looked at her hands as they brushed out the woman's hair.

"Do you think she's pretty, Charley? I always figured she was. She still is, even now. Don't you think?"

My head was spinning. "What do you mean, his wife? You were his wife."

She nodded slowly.

"Yes, I was."

"You can't have two wives."

"No," she whispered. "You're right. You can't."

ℝ THE WOMAN SNIFFED. Her eyes looked red and tired. She didn't acknowledge me. But she seemed to be listening as my mother spoke.

"I think your father got scared during the war. He didn't know how long it would last. A lot of men were killed in those mountains. Maybe she gave him security. Maybe he thought he'd never get home. Who knows? He always needed a plan, your father, he said that a lot: 'Have a plan. Have a plan.'"

"I don't understand," I said. "Dad wrote you that letter."

"Yes."

"He proposed. You accepted."

She sighed. "When he realized the war was ending, I guess he wanted a different plan—his old plan, with me. Things change when you're not in danger anymore, Charley. And so—" She lifted the woman's hair from her shoulders. "He left her behind."

She paused.

"Your father had a knack for that."

I shook my head. "But why did you—"

"He never told me, Charley. He never told anyone. But at some point, over the years, he found her again. Or she found him. And eventually, he brought her to America. He set up a whole other life. He even bought a second house. In Collingswood. Where he built his new store, remember?"

The woman put the brush down. My mother's hands

withdrew and she hooked them together now, bringing them under her chin.

"It was her ziti your father wanted me to make all those years." She sighed. "For some reason, that still bugs me."

⧉ AND THEN SHE told me the rest of the story. How she discovered all this. How she asked once why they never got a bill from the hotel in Collingswood. How he said he was paying cash, which made her suspicious. How she arranged for a babysitter one Friday night, then drove nervously to Collingswood herself, going up and down the streets, until she saw his Buick in the driveway of a strange house, and she burst into tears.

"I was shaking, Charley. I had to force every step. I snuck down to a window and looked inside. They were eating dinner. Your father had his shirt unbuttoned, his undershirt showing, like he always did with us. He was sitting with his food, no hurry, relaxed, as if he lived there, passing the dishes to this woman and . . ."

She stopped.

"Are you sure you want to know this?"

I nodded blankly.

"Their son."

"What . . . ?"

"He was a few years older than you."

"A . . . boy?"

My voice squeaked as I said that.

"I'm sorry, Charley."

I felt dizzy, as if falling backward. Even telling you now, I have trouble getting the words out. My father, who had demanded my devotion, my loyalty to his team, *our* team, the men in our family. He had another *son*?

"Did he play baseball?" I whispered.

My mother looked at me helplessly.

"Charley," she said, almost crying, "I really don't know."

കൃ THE WOMAN IN the bathrobe opened a small drawer. She took out some papers and flipped through them. Was she really who my mother said she was? She looked Italian. She seemed the right age. I tried to picture my father meeting her. I tried to picture them together. I didn't know a thing about this woman or this apartment, but I felt my old man all over the room.

"I drove home that night, Charley," my mother said, "and I sat on the curb. I waited. I didn't even want him pulling in to our driveway. He came back after midnight and I'll never forget the look on his face when the headlights hit me, because in that moment, I think he knew he'd been found out.

"I got into the car and I made him roll up all the windows. I didn't want anyone hearing me. And then I exploded. I exploded in such a way that he couldn't use any of his lies. He finally admitted who she was, where they had met, what he'd been trying to do. My head was spinning. My stomach hurt so badly, I couldn't sit up straight. You expect a lot of things in a marriage, Charley, but who could see themselves *replaced* like that?"

She turned to the wall, her gaze falling on the painting of the vineyards.

"I'm not sure it really hit me until months later. Inside that car, I was just furious. And heartbroken. He swore he was sorry. He swore he didn't know about this other son, that when he found out, he felt obligated to do something. I don't know what was true and what wasn't. Even screaming, your father had an answer for everything.

"But none of it mattered. It was over. Don't you see? I could have forgiven him almost anything against me. But that was a betrayal of you and your sister, too."

She turned to me.

"You have one family, Charley. For good or bad. You have one family. You can't trade them in. You can't lie to them. You can't run two at once, substituting back and forth.

"Sticking with your family is what *makes* it a family."

She sighed.

"So I had to make a decision."

I tried to picture that awful moment. In a car, after midnight, with the windows rolled up—from the outside, two figures silently screaming. I tried to picture how our family slept in one house while another family slept in another, and both had my father's clothes hanging in the closet.

I tried to picture charming Posey of Pepperville Beach

losing her old life that night, crying and screaming as it all collapsed in front of her. And I realized that, on the list of Times My Mother Stood Up for Me, this would have to go at the top.

"Mom," I finally whispered, "what did you tell him?"

"I told him to leave. And to never come back."

So now I knew what happened the night before the corn puffs.

*T*HERE ARE MANY THINGS in my life that I wish I could take back. Many moments I would recast. But the one I would change if I could change just one would not be for me but for my daughter, Maria, who came looking for her grandmother that Sunday afternoon and found her sprawled on the bedroom floor. She tried to wake her. She started screaming. She raced in and out of the room, torn between yelling for help and not leaving her alone. That never should have happened. She was only a kid.

I think from that point on, it was hard for me to face my daughter or my wife. I think that's why I drank so much. I think that's why I whimpered off into another life, because deep down I didn't feel that I deserved the old one anymore. I ran away. In that manner, I suppose, my father and I were sadly parallel. When, two weeks later, in the quiet of our bedroom, I confessed to Catherine where I had been, that there was no business trip, that I was playing baseball in a Pittsburgh stadium while my mother lay dying, she was more numb than anything else. She kept looking as if she wanted to say something that she never ended up saying.

In the end, her only comment was, "At this point, what does it matter?"

⟋⟍ MY MOTHER CROSSED the small bedroom and stood by the only window. She moved the curtains aside.

"It's dark out," she said.

Behind us, at the mirror, the Italian woman looked down, fingering her papers.

"Mom?" I said. "Do you hate her?"

She shook her head. "Why should I hate her? She only wanted the same things I did. She didn't get them, either. Their marriage ended. Your father moved on. Like I said, he had a knack for that."

She grabbed her elbows, as if she were cold. The woman at the mirror put her face in her hands. She let out a small sob.

"Secrets, Charley," my mother whispered. "They'll tear you apart."

We all three hung there silently for a minute, each in our own world. Then my mother turned to me.

"You have to go now," she said.

"Go?" My voice choked. "Where? Why?"

"But Charley . . ." She took my hands. "I want to ask you something first."

Her eyes were wet with tears.

"Why do you want to die?"

I shivered. For a second I couldn't breathe.

"You knew . . . ?"

She gave a sad smile.

"I'm your mother."

My body convulsed. I spit out a gush of air. "Mom.... I'm not who you think...I messed things up. I drank. I blew everything. I lost my family..."

"No, Charley—"

"Yes, yes, I did." My voice was shaking. "I fell apart.... Catherine's gone, Mom. I drove her away....Maria, I'm not even in her life ...she's married...I wasn't even there...I'm an outsider now...I'm an outsider to everything I loved...."

My chest was heaving. "And you...that last day....I never should have left you... I could never tell you ..."

My head lowered in shame.

"...how sorry...how I'm so...so..."

That was all I got out. I fell to the floor, sobbing uncontrollably, emptying myself, wailing. The room shrunk to a heat behind my eyes. I don't know how long I was like that. When I found my voice, it was barely a rasp.

"I wanted it to stop, Mom...this anger, this guilt. That's why...I wanted to die..."

I lifted my eyes, and, for the first time, admitted the truth.

"I gave up," I whispered.

"Don't give up," she whispered back.

I buried my head then. I am not ashamed to say it. I buried my head in my mother's arms and her hands cradled my neck. We held each other like that, just briefly. But I cannot put into words the comfort I drew from that moment. I can only say that, as I speak to you now, I still yearn for it.

"I wasn't there when you died, Mom."

"You had something to do."

"I lied. It was the worst lie I ever told. . . . It wasn't work. I went to play in a game . . . a stupid game. . . . I was so desperate to please—"

"Your father."

She nodded gently.

And I realized she had known all along.

Across the room, the Italian woman pulled her bathrobe tighter. She clasped her hands as if in prayer. Such a strange trio we made, each of us, at some point, longing to be loved by the same man. I could still hear his words, forcing my decision: *mama's boy or daddy's boy, Chick? What's it gonna be?*

"I made the wrong choice," I whispered.

My mother shook her head.

"A child should never have to choose."

&ø THE ITALIAN WOMAN stood up now. She wiped her eyes and collected herself. She placed her fingers on the edge of the dressing table and pushed two items close together. My mother motioned me forward until I could see what she had been looking at.

One was a photo of a young man in a graduation cap. I assume it was her son.

The other was my baseball card.

She flicked her eyes up to the mirror and caught our reflections, the three of us, framed like a bizarre family portrait. For the first and only moment, I was certain she saw me.

"Perdonare," the woman mumbled.

And everything around us disappeared.

Chick Finishes His Story

*H*AVE YOU EVER ISOLATED your earliest childhood memory? Mine is when I was three years old. It was summer. A carnival in the park near our house. There were balloons and cotton candy stands. A bunch of guys who had just finished a tug-of-war were lined up at the water fountain.

I must have been thirsty, because my mother lifted me by my armpits and carried me to the front of that line. And I remember how she cut in front of those sweaty, shirtless men, how she squeezed one arm tight around my chest and used her free hand to turn the handle. She whispered in my ear, "Drink the water, Charley," and I bent forward, my feet dangling above the ground, and I slurped it up, and all those men just waited for us to finish. I can still feel her arm around me. I can still see the bubbling water. That is my earliest memory, mother and son, a world unto ourselves.

Now, at the end of this last day together, the same thing was happening. My body felt broken. I could barely make it move. But her arm went across my chest and I sensed her carrying me once more, air passing over my face. I saw only darkness, as if we were traveling behind the length of a curtain. Then the dark pulled away and there were stars. Thousands of them. She was laying me down in wet grass, returning my ruined soul to this world.

"Mom . . ." My throat was raw. I had to swallow between words. "That woman . . . ? What was she saying?"

She gently lowered my shoulders. "Forgive."

"Forgive her? Dad?"

My head touched the earth. I felt moist blood trickling down my temples.

"Yourself," she said.

My body was locking up. I couldn't move my arms or legs. I was slipping away. How much time did I have left?

"Yes," I rasped.

She looked confused.

"Yes, you were a good mother."

She touched her mouth to hide a grin, and she seemed to fill to bursting.

"Live," she said.

"No, wait—"

"I love you, Charley."

She waved her fingertips. I was crying.

"I'll lose you . . ."

Her face seemed to float over mine.

"You can't lose your mother, Charley. I'm right here."

Then a huge flash of light obliterated her image.

"CHARLES BENETTO. CAN YOU HEAR ME?"

I felt a tingling in my limbs.

"WE'RE GOING TO MOVE YOU NOW."

I wanted to pull her back.

"ARE YOU WITH US, CHARLES?"

"Me and my mother," I mumbled.

I felt a soft kiss on my forehead.

"My mother and I," she corrected.

And she was gone.

☙ I BLINKED HARD. I saw the sky. I saw the stars. Then the stars began to fall. They grew larger as they grew closer, round and white, like baseballs, and I instinctively opened my palms as if widening my glove to catch them all.

"WAIT. LOOK AT HIS HANDS!"

The voice softened.

"CHARLES?"

Even softer.

"Charles . . . ? Hey, there you go, fella. Come back to us . . . YO! GUYS!"

He waved his flashlight at two other police officers. He was young, just as I had thought.

Chick's Final Thoughts

*N*OW, AS I SAID when you first sat down, I don't expect you to go with me here. I haven't told this story before, but I had hoped to. I waited for this chance. And I'm glad it's come, now that it's done.

I have forgotten so many things in my life, yet I can remember every moment of that time with my mother, the people we saw, the things we discussed. It was so ordinary in so many ways, but as she said, you can find something truly important in an ordinary minute. You may think me crazy, that I imagined the whole thing. But I believe this in the deepest part of my soul: My mother, somewhere between this world and the next, gave me one more day, the day I'd wanted so badly, and she told me all that I've told you.

And if my mother said it, I believe it.

"What causes an echo?" she once quizzed me.

The persistence of sound after the source has stopped.

"When can you hear an echo?"

When it's quiet and other sounds are absorbed.

When it's quiet, I can hear my mother's echo still.

I feel ashamed now that I tried to take my life. It is such a precious thing. I had no one to talk me out of my despair, and that was a mistake. You need to keep people close. You need to give them access to your heart.

As for what's happened in the two years since, there are so many details: the hospital stay, the treatment I received, where I've been. Let's just say, for now, that I was lucky on many levels. I'm alive. I didn't kill anyone. I have been sober every day since—although some days are harder than others.

I've thought a lot about that night. I believe my mother saved my life. I also believe that parents, if they love you, will hold you up safely, above their swirling waters, and sometimes that means you'll never know what they endured, and you may treat them unkindly, in a way you otherwise wouldn't.

But there's a story behind everything. How a picture got on a wall. How a scar got on your face. Sometimes the stories are simple, and sometimes they are hard and heartbreaking. But behind all your stories is always your mother's story, because hers is where yours begins.

So this was my mother's story.

And mine.

I would like to make things right again with those I love.

Epilogue

CHARLES "CHICK" BENETTO died last month, five years after his attempted suicide, and three years after our encounter on that Saturday morning.

The funeral was small, only a few family members— including his ex-wife—and several friends from his childhood in Pepperville Beach, who recalled climbing a water tower with Chick and spray-painting their names on the tank. No one from his baseball days was on hand, although the Pittsburgh Pirates sent a condolence card.

His father was there. He stood in the back of the church, a slim man with stooped shoulders and thin white hair. He wore a brown suit and sunglasses, and left quickly after the service.

The cause of Chick's death was a sudden stroke, an embolism that went to his brain and killed him almost instantly. Doctors speculate that his blood vessels may have weakened from the head trauma of his car crash. He was fifty-eight when he died. Too young, everyone agreed.

As for the details of his "story"? In putting this account together, I checked into nearly all of them. There was, indeed, an accident on the highway entrance ramp that night, and a car, after clipping the front end of a moving van, went over an embankment, destroyed a billboard, and ejected its driver into the grass.

There was, indeed, a widow named Rose Templeton, who lived on Lehigh Street in Pepperville Beach and died shortly after the accident. There was also a Miss Thelma Bradley, who died not long after, and whose obituary in the local newspaper identified her as "a retired housekeeper."

A marriage certificate was filed in 1962—a year after the Benettos divorced—for a Leonard Benetto and a Gianna Tusicci, confirming an earlier marriage in Italy. A Leo Tusicci, presumably their son, was listed as a student at Collingswood High School in the early 1960s. There were no other records for him.

As for Pauline "Posey" Benetto? She died of a heart attack at age seventy-nine, and the details of her life match the accounts given in these pages. Her humor, warmth, and motherly wisdom were attested to by her surviving family. Her photo still hangs at the beauty parlor where she worked. In it, she is wearing a blue smock and hoop earrings.

Chick Benetto's final years seemed to bring him some contentment. He sold his mother's home in Pepperville Beach and directed the proceeds to his daughter. He later moved to an apartment to be near her, and they reestablished a relationship, including Saturday morning "donut runs" in which they caught up on events of the week over coffee and crullers. Although he never fully reconciled with Catherine Benetto, they made their peace and spoke regularly.

His salesman days were over, but until his death, Chick worked part-time with a local parks and recreation office, where he had one rule for the organized games: Everyone gets to play.

A week before his stroke, he seemed to sense that his time was short. He told those around him, "Remember me for these days, not the old ones."

He was buried in a plot near his mother.

BECAUSE THERE WAS a ghost involved, you may call this a ghost story. But what family isn't a ghost story? Sharing tales of those we've lost is how we keep from really losing them.

And even though Chick is gone now, his story flows through others. It flows through me. I don't think he was crazy. I think he really did get one more day with his mother. And one day spent with someone you love can change everything.

I know. I had a day like that, too, in the bleachers of a Little League field—a day to listen, to love, to apologize, to forgive. And to decide, years later, that this baby boy I am carrying will soon be called, proudly, Charley.

My married name is Maria Lang.

But before that I was Maria Benetto.

Chick Benetto was my father.

And if my father said it, I believe it.

Acknowledgments

The author would like to thank Leslie Wells and Will Schwalbe for their editing; Bob Miller for his patience and belief; Ellen Archer, Jane Comins, Katie Wainright, Christine Ragasa, SallyAnne McCartin, Sarah Schaffer, and Maha Khalil for their tireless support; Phil Rose for his wonderful art; and Miriam Wenger and David Lott for their keen eyes. Special thanks to Kerri Alexander, who still handles everything; to David Black, who buoyed me through countless chicken dinners; and especially to Janine, who heard this story on quiet mornings, read aloud, and gave it its first smile. And of course, as this is a story about family—to my family, those before me, those after me, and those all around me.

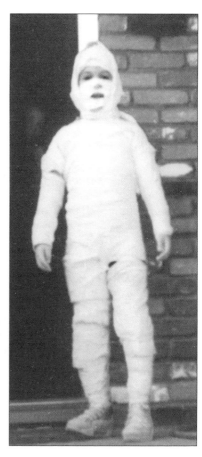

This book is dedicated, with love, to Rhoda Albom, the mommy of the mummy